W9-BZX-502

BEST
GAY EROTICA
2014

BEST GAY EROTICA 2014

Series Editor
LARRY DUPLECHAN

Selected and Introduced by
JOE MANNETTI

CLEiS
PRESS

Copyright © 2013 by Larry Duplechan.
Introduction copyright © 2013 by Joe Mannetti.

All rights reserved. Except for brief passages quoted in newspaper, magazine, radio, television or online reviews, no part of this book may be reproduced in any form or by any means, electronic or mechanical, including photocopying, recording, or information storage or retrieval system, without permission in writing from the Publisher.

Published in the United States by Cleis Press Inc., 2246 Sixth Street, Berkeley, California 94710.

Printed in the United States.
Cover design: Scott Idleman/Blink
Cover photograph: Geber86/Getty Images
Text design: Frank Wiedemann
First Edition.
10 9 8 7 6 5 4 3 2 1

Trade paper ISBN: 978-1-62778-001-8
E-book ISBN: 978-1-62778-014-8

Grateful acknowledgment is made to the following for granting permission to reprint copyrighted material: "Steam Punk," by Eric Del Carlo, originally appeared in *Steam Bath,* edited by Shane Allison (Cleis Press, 2013); "Five-Finger Discount," © 2012 by Huck Pilgrim, reprinted (in slightly different form) from an Amazon Kindle Edition (2012); "The One in the Middle," © 2012 by Dominic Santi, reprinted (in slightly different form) with the author's permission from *Middle Men,* edited by Shane Allison (Cleis Press, 2012); "My Best Friend's Dad," by J. M. Snyder, originally appeared in *Show-Offs,* edited by Richard Labonté (Cleis Press, 2013).

CONTENTS

FOREWORD

I would not have imagined six months ago that I would end up editing *Best Gay Erotica 2014*, but now that I'm here, it feels surprisingly inevitable. The week before Thanksgiving, 2012, Brenda Knight (Publisher of Cleis Press) emailed me concerning an essay of mine, "Bigchest: Confessions of a Tit Man," which had appeared in *Muscle Men: Rock Hard Gay Erotica* (Cleis Press, 2010), and which Brenda hoped to reprint in *Best Gay Erotica 2013*. I had "guest judged" *BGE 2012* for Richard Labonté, editor of the series since 1995. When I asked why she (rather than Richard) had contacted me, Ms. Knight informed me that Richard had decided to end his run as editor of the *Best Gay Erotica* series.

I have known Richard Labonté since the mid-1980s: he wrote the first (to my knowledge) review of my first novel (*Eight Days A Week*) in 1985, in *In Touch for Men Magazine*; and has been a long-distance buddy and Larry Duplechan booster ever since. I gave Ms. Knight permission to reprint my essay; and she, in turn, asked if I might be interested in editing *Best Gay Erotica*

2014. I invited her to phone me, and a few minutes of discussion later, I said yes.

Which left me with some mighty big shoes to fill: Richard Labonté has edited shelves of anthologies for Cleis, including, of course, sixteen annual editions of *Best Gay Erotica*. Few could balance literary quality and sheer filthiness with such dexterity. Fortunately, I would not have to face this task alone. Before contracting me for this anthology, Cleis requested I send them a short list of candidates to serve as guest judge. Happily, my first choice was also the publishers' first choice. Even more happily, that choice was another buddy of mine: LGBT activist, former erotic-video performer and current sexy hunk of man-meat Joe Mannetti. I've known Joe for over twenty years, having met him sometime in the early 1990s at a reading given at the now-defunct A Different Light Bookstore in the Silver Lake area of Los Angeles, where Joe had admired my writing and I had admired Joe's amazing chest. We have been friends, and shared a mutual letch, ever since (I have long held that a bit of sexual tension only helps keep a friendship interesting).

Thank you, Joe, for doing so much of the heavy lifting— fortunately, you do have the shoulders for it. Thanks also to the writers whose stories appear here, and to the many fine writers to whom I finally had to say no thank you. Thanks to Jason A. Quest for his eye-popping artwork. And thanks to Cleis Press (namely, Felice and Brenda) for taking a chance on a newbie. I've given it my best shot, and as I've said, I had some mighty big shoes to fill.

Larry Duplechan
Los Angeles, California

INTRODUCTION

Those who are easily shocked should be shocked more often.

—Mae West

Those are words to live by, from an iconic woman who really knew how to live.

My name is Joe Mannetti. I grew up in New York before heading out west to spend more than two decades living in Los Angeles, California, pursuing the limelight of Hollywood. My journey to the land of all that glitters included coming out as a loud and proud gay man, which led to connecting with the Bear and Leather communities, which led to entering several contests and winning five Bear titles (including Mr. International Daddy Bear 2009), which led to more than a couple of nude pictorials, which led to a brief career as a performer in the "jizz biz," which led to here. Of course, there were a few other accomplishments along the way. But, truth be told, it's the sex that sells.

When folks remember me, it's usually for all those naked photo spreads in which I bared all, and those Bear vids in which I did it all—or had it done to me. That's probably what prompted my L.A. bud, award-winning and prolific author Larry Duplechan, to ask me to guest-judge *Best Gay Erotica 2014*. I was flattered, and I welcomed the opportunity to embrace the celebration of raw testosterone, kink and masculine sexuality that the stories you will read here reveal on every page.

In this book, we present a tasty assortment of short tales that revel in the smells, sounds, shapes and sensations of men enjoying sex with other men. We start out with a sweaty encounter initiated by a power outage in Lee Hitt's "The Power Man," followed by a game of cards that leads to the most exciting gamble two men can enjoy winning together in "Gambling with Harvey," by Tony Haynes. Landon Dixon takes us on a hedonistic journey with a man who knows how to please everybody he services in "Everybody's Boy," then comes a kinky game filled with enjoyable torture as Boot LS shows us the ropes in "The Piñata Conquest." Shane Allison gives us a preview of coming attractions at the porn shop in "Big Thick Dick and Double-Chocolate Bubble Booty." And there's more manly mischief from authors K. Lynn, Calvin Gimpelevich, Huck Pilgrim, J. M. Snyder, Eric Del Carlo, David Holly, Dilo Keith, Gregory L. Norris, Jay Starre, Dominic Santi, Thomas Fuchs, Dan Cavanagh, Dale Lazarov and Max Vos; and ace comic book artist Jason A. Quest. Each contributor invites us to explore every ripple and nipple, every grunt and groan of men getting it on with other men and enjoying every musky moment of it. These nineteen stories give you a chance to escape into the world of man-on-man hotness. Larry and I hope this collection has something for everyone who digs men and the intimacies that they can share together.

In deciding which selections to insert between the covers of this latest edition of gay male erotica, I used a scale suggested by our studly editor: one-to-five stars (for literary merit) and one-to-five boners (for sheer nastiness). Every story included here gave Joe a rise, and that's why every one of them made it inside—the book. I invite you to allow them to penetrate your innermost fantasies, and enjoy the release that going there produces. I know I did.

The experience of man-on-man sex is as diverse as the men who engage in it. It can be sweet and hot with someone you know and love, but, as some wise soul once stated, "Even with someone you *don't* know, it can be wonderful!"

So here's to all the tricks who turn out to be real treats, the hunks who enjoy exploring their horniness and the studs who celebrate gay sex. My own journey of sexual freedom has connected me to most of the good things and even the highest achievements, professionally and personally, in my life. As I went from contest winner to pin-up, porn performer to writer, and on to actor and even LGBT outreach advocate, the power of sex has always been there guiding me. It still inspires me, and I hope you will allow it to inspire you. As another iconic sex symbol once pointed out,

> *We are all born sexual creatures, thank God, but it's a pity so many people despise and crush this natural gift.*
>
> —Marilyn Monroe

Here's to embracing that natural gift. Enjoy!

Joe Mannetti
Connecticut

THE POWER MAN

Lee Hitt

My power is out. I'm not sure exactly when it happened. Or how. I'm not even sure what time it is now. Judging by the beam of sunlight streaming through the slit in the thick curtains, my guess is that it's daytime. I pull back the curtains and squint through the glass. Looks like the power lines outside my house went down. Some lie limp on the street, others sag power-lessly from the lines or from branches. They must have been blown down by heavy winds. The yard is wet from the night's pounding rain, but the pavement already looks dry. Just looking at the street, I'd never know it had rained.

I click on the battery-operated radio. They say it could be days before the power comes back on. Then the radio dies, the voice first becoming crackly, then dimming to a distant whisper and finally fading to silence altogether.

I shuffle into the kitchen to make coffee, and flick the light switch. Nothing. Oh, that's right: the power is out. It's so easy to forget when the power is out. It's usually always there, readily accessible. Flick a switch and let there be light.

Then one day, it isn't.

There won't be any coffee today, either, I realize as I turned the knob on the electric stove top. No heat, no coffee.

I go back into the bedroom. Stupidly, I flick that light switch, too. I have to stop doing that, flicking switches and hoping something happens. But we've all been conditioned to do it, to think we have power over the power.

After drawing the curtains tight, blocking out all the light, I burrow under my blankets and go back to sleep.

I wake up sweaty and emerge from my cocoon of blankets hot and horny. The air conditioner has been off for who knows how many hours. I glance at the digital clock on the bedside table. Its face is blank. I could have been out for days. I have no idea. It doesn't matter though. I'm horny. At least I can control that.

That's the beauty of working from home. I get to do what I want, when I want. Well, most of the time, anyway. Without power, I'm not going to get much done. I can work from my laptop when the power is off, but then I'm on a time limit. The little meter in the corner of the screen counts down the hours until blackout. It's too much pressure.

I find my vibrating butt plug, a plump little purple number, in the dresser's bottom drawer. Lying on my back atop the sweaty sheets, my knees against my ribs, I squeeze the firm rubber digit into my eager hole and flick the switch. Nothing. It just sits there, lifeless, protruding from my asshole like a little purple cork.

Using rechargeable batteries in my anal vibe doesn't usually pose a problem. Only today I can't recharge them. Today, it's out of my control.

A sharp crack in the yard startles me, and I scurry to the

window with the purple plug still up my ass. I stick my head between the thick curtains and look through the window.

There are men in my yard.

The power lines are no longer on the ground, no longer dangling from leaning poles. I hope the power comes back on soon. My whole day has been thrown off. Once my routine is screwed up, the rest of my day is shot.

Someone knocks at my door. I pull on a robe and shuffle down the hallway. The thin carpet feels scratchy beneath my bare soles.

It's the power man. His sleeves are rolled up to his elbows. His forearms are sweaty. His *everything* is sweaty. A dark *U*-shaped stain drips down the front of his chest. A wet circle blooms under each armpit. I glance down, quickly, and see a faint dark shadow between his legs. I look back up and see that his eyes, electric blue, haven't left my face.

"I was wondering if your power was back on," he says through full lips and a thick beard.

"No. It hasn't come back on yet."

"We're not sure what the problem is. We've fixed the lines. Everything looks good outside."

"Must be a problem inside," I say.

"Must be."

A pause. Near-tangible quiet hangs in the air, like static electricity.

"I'll have to call someone to look at it, I guess," I say.

"I can take a quick look," he says. "If you want."

"Sure, sure, come on in."

He steps inside.

"At least it's a little cooler in here," he says. He looks around the dark room. Keeping the curtains closed keeps the temperature down. The room is lit only by the corona of light around the edges of the curtains, and through the slit in the middle. The power man's pupils dilate, adjusting to the dark.

"Do you want some water or something?" I ask. "You look pretty hot."

"Yeah, thanks," he says. He takes off his cap and wipes the sweat from his brow with his forearm. The dark hairs on his arm stick down in a dark streak, plastered with sweat.

As I fill a glass with water and a few misshapen, half-melted ice cubes, he unbuttons the top button of his shirt. Then the second, exposing a white undershirt. It's soaked through with sweat, almost clear. Thick chest hairs push against the fabric.

"Here you go," I say, bringing him the glass of water. Beads of sweat are already starting to condense on the outside of the glass. He takes it and downs it in one deep swallow. He wipes the cool condensation from his hand through his short hair.

"Do you want another?" I ask.

"If I have another, I might stay in here all day. I should go check out your fuse box."

I lead him to the fuse box, in the laundry room. "I'll leave you to it, I guess," I say.

"It'll just take a minute," he says. "You can stay here." He punches the latch with his thick index finger, popping it up, and yanks the fuse-box door open.

The laundry room is small and stuffy. I haven't put a curtain on the small window high up on the wall. A rectangle of light, bright and hot, shines on the dryer. I rest my hand on the metal surface of the dryer: it's so hot, I snatch my hand away quickly.

I can smell the power man, his musk mingling with the scents of laundry detergent and dryer sheets. I like his scent better. I wish I could wash my clothes in his scent, wash myself in it.

I twitch under my bathrobe. I turn away from him, facing the dryer, and act as though I'm straightening the bottles of cleaning supplies on the shelf. I undo the tie of my bathroom and retie it, strapping my stiff dick to my stomach.

"You've blown a fuse," the power man says.

I turn around, speechless, my cock throbbing against the bathrobe tie.

"I don't think that's the whole problem, but it's a start. I've got a spare in the truck. Be right back." He places his hot hand on my waist and sidles around me to exit the laundry room. I slump against the corner of the dryer like a horny fifties housewife. But the dryer isn't on. The power is still out.

He's gone for a long time. He's probably not coming back.

In the kitchen, I fill another glass with water and ice. It sits on the counter, waiting for the power man to return.

A wet ring spreads on the counter. I run a finger through the moisture on the countertop and run a cool fingertip across my forehead.

The door creaks open. The power man lets himself back in. The smell of his wet musk precedes him, this time mingled with tobacco smoke. He must have taken a smoke break.

"This will only take a minute," he says, and brushes by me. He ignores the glass on the counter, the wet ring puddling across the laminate.

My dick goes soft and slips out from under the bathrobe tie. It hangs powerless between my legs.

I can hear him clanking around the laundry room, and I crane my neck to get a better look. He produces a screwdriver from the belt around his waist and fiddles with something, pops out the fuse, replaces it. Just like that. With his thumb, he flicks the heavy switch on the fuse from left to right.

Nothing happens. He flicks the switch from right to left. Left to right. Still nothing.

He grunts. "I don't know what the problem is, man." He comes back into the kitchen. He has the dead fuse tucked into the palm of his hand. "Is that for me?" he asks, tilting his head toward the glass of water sweating on the counter.

I nod.

He sets the dead switch on the counter and picks up the glass of water. Again, he downs it in one gulp, this one slower, though. Deeper. I pick up the dead fuse as he drinks and flick the switch back and forth. *Click. Click.*

"Flicking that's not going to fix anything," he says, his eyes never leaving mine. Droplets of water cling to his beard.

Before I can turn around and hide it, my cock rises up, right between the panels of my bathrobe. Its exposed head, a clear bead of juice clinging to the tip, points right at the power man.

"That's not going to fix anything either," he says.

I go red and turn away from him, reaching under my bathrobe and again tying my cock around my waist.

"Don't," he says, coming up behind me. His wet beard rasps against my earlobe.

With a quick movement, he wraps his hands around my waist and undoes the tie of my bathrobe. My cock pops out and smacks against the counter with a heavy thwack.

I turn around, and the power man steps backward, away from me. He nimbly undoes his buttons with his thick fingers and slips his sweaty work shirt from his shoulders. His white undershirt is sleeveless. His nipples are dark and hard against the wet fabric. His pit hair drips with sweat. The aroma of musk and smoke fills my nostrils and I get even harder.

Taking the back of my head in his large hand, he pulls me into him, smothering my face in his wet pit. Thirsty for his sweat, I lick it. Feel it run down my throat. The damp hairs brush against my lips, my cheeks, my chin. My cock throbs.

He grabs my hair and pulls my face away from his armpit. I run a finger along my own cheek and smell it. My face smells like him.

I struggle to keep up as he drags me by one arm down the dark hallway. He throws open the door to the bathroom, another door to a closet, before finding the bedroom at the end of the hall. He throws me onto the bed, peels his shirt off. Undoes his belt buckle; lets his pants fall to the floor. He's not wearing underwear. His hard cock bounces up and down as he crosses the floor toward the bed. I lean into him, my mouth open, hungry. He puts his hand across my face and pushes me backward onto the bed. After he strips off my robe, he pulls my legs apart, wide. My balls hang low between my legs.

He grunts, the same noise he made when the flicked the fuse switch and nothing happened.

"What's this?" he asks, pushing my legs farther apart. He holds one leg down with his arm, the other with a socked foot. His free hand reaches between my legs. With a finger, he brushes the purple butt plug in my ass. Static electricity discharges from his fingertip. The vibrator comes back to life.

The vibrations, stronger than I can ever remember them being, fill my hole with an electric tingle that surges into my gut. My cock jumps. I open my mouth and moan. My mouth is barely open a second before he's on top of me, shoving his hard cock between my lips. I feel its swollen head press against the back of my throat.

He takes the bathrobe tie and wraps it around my head, around his waist. He ties my head to him, so that I have no choice but to be filled with his cock. I grab a handful of ass in each hand. My nose is buried in his dark, thick bush. All I can see are the hairs on his belly, a narrow trail marching from navel to crotch. The smell of his thick pubic bush, ripe with sweat, is intoxicating. His precum tastes sweet on my tongue. All my senses are filled with him.

Reaching behind himself, he finds my dick and pumps it. It is dripping, too. He runs his thumb through my precum, flicks the pad of his thumb across my piss slit, left and right, right and left. An electric shock runs through my prick. My body trembles. His cock stifles my moan.

"I want to hear you moan," he says, and he unties my head. His wet dick slides out of my mouth with a moist pop. He grips my dick, and I moan.

"Louder," he says, squeezing my dick in his strong fist. I moan louder. I can taste him on my tongue.

He presses his other pit over my mouth. I struggle to breathe, only able to swallow his scent, his sweat. He strokes my dick faster. The head, dark purple and swollen, feels like it's going to explode. My body tingles, surging with an electric charge.

He pushes me flat against the bed and sits on my face. His hot balls hang down into my open mouth. Slick with my spit, his dick slides along my face, flicking my nose, left and right, right and left, then bounces up and down, while his balls rest on my wet lips.

Leaning back, he rubs me to completion. The pleasure over-flows, filling my entire body with a rolling spasm. My cockhead swells one last time and explodes, spraying a hot stream of jizz onto my belly, onto his back.

He raises up on his knees and runs a finger through the thick puddle on my belly. It coats his finger like glue. He rubs it into his armpit hair, and it clings there, sticky and white.

"Suck it off," he says, pressing his smelly pit covered in my own cum over my face. I slurp my own sweet cum, mixed with the tang of his sweat. As I suck his pit hair clean, I feel his finger along my belly, gathering up the rest of my cum. When he removes his pit from my face, I see that he's been coating his own cock with it.

"Suck it off," he says again, shoving his cock in my mouth. "Get it nice and slick, because I'm going to fuck you," he says, sliding his cock in and out between my lips. "This is all the lube you get." When his dick is slippery with my spit and cum, he pulls it out of my mouth and flips me over. He uncorks the plug from my ass and tosses it onto the floor. It slowly vibrates across the floor for a couple of seconds before giving up and slowing to a stop. I imagine it, like me, gasping for air.

His fat, wet cockhead presses against my hole. The pressure makes my whole body surge. My skin ripples with electricity. I moan into the pillow.

"Louder," he says. I moan louder. He reaches around my chest and grabs my nipples between his fingers. Pinching hard, he shoves his cock deep into my hole.

He plugs it in. It fills me completely.

The lights come on. The clock flashes *12:00*. Even the little butt plug on the floor gives one last vibration and scoots a good inch across the carpet.

The power man erupts into my hole. His body seems to collapse in upon itself like a spent supernova, and he falls onto me, panting.

The air conditioner rumbles to life. The power man raises himself up, his hot, wet skin peeling away from mine. Cool air hits the sweat on my back. I watch the power man in the mirror. His flesh ripples; his nipples harden.

The power man leans down, his face next to mine. His lips just brush my earlobe. I feel cool air on my lower back, his hot breath in my ear. He says, "Your power's fixed."

He gets up. I hear the rustle of clothing and the sound of the front door. Open. Close.

I roll onto my back, my legs spread, his juice leaking out onto the sheets.

I trace my fingertips along my body. My face. The racing pulse in my throat. My own hard nipples. My hip bones. The tops of my thighs.

I see sparks.

GAMBLING WITH HARVEY

Tony Haynes

Kris studied his hand thoughtfully. It was a mess. Five random cards, the highest of which was a king. Harvey glanced across at him and smiled. Kris wondered whether to simply give in, lean across the table and plant a kiss on Harvey's adorable lips. As well as having the looks of an old-fashioned movie idol, Harvey exuded charm, charisma and a certain roguish quality that made him nigh on irresistible to both men and women alike. Harvey took a long drag upon the cigarette he was smoking. "Taking an awfully long time, old chap. I think it's about time you made a decision."

Harvey reached across with his left hand and lightly brushed the back of Kris's right. Kris closed his eyes momentarily. He found Harvey's touch electric. He gulped, shook Harvey's hand away and made up his mind to go on with the game. At least if he won, it would give him a modicum of control over the situation. He was just about to reply when the door behind him opened and Pippa strolled in, her hips swaying provocatively as she did so. As if sensing the import of the moment, Pippa didn't say anything. She topped up the boys' drinks, gave Harvey a cheeky wink and then left them to it. Finally, Kris made a decision. He cleared his throat and said, "I'll take three."

Very slowly, very deliberately, Harvey dealt Kris three cards from the deck he was holding. As Kris picked them up, it was all he could do to stop himself from laughing aloud. It seemed as if his luck was in after all, for he now held an eight, two tens and two kings.

Harvey studied Kris for a moment before discarding two cards and dealing himself two others from the deck. Harvey glanced down at his new hand. Kris didn't think that it was a particularly confident look. Harvey treated Kris to another of those incredibly feline smiles. "So, call it."

Kris lay his cards down on the table. "Two pairs. Kings and tens."

Harvey clicked his fingers. "Damn."

Kris smiled broadly. "I thought you said you never lost."

Harvey shrugged. "Ah well, guess you can't win them all."

"So what did you have?" Kris asked, intrigued.

"You really want to see?"

Kris nodded eagerly. Harvey gestured at the five cards he had abandoned facedown on the table. Kris turned them over one by one. The first card was an ace, the second a jack, the third a nine. Kris was almost starting to feel sorry for his dashing acquaintance; only the fourth card he turned over was another ace. Kris felt his pulse rate quicken as he reached for the final card. As his fingers bent back the edge, the knave of hearts peeked up at him. Kris's hand began to tremble ever so slightly. "You...you..."

"Spit it out."

Kris couldn't. For a second he panicked, but then he took a

deep breath and looked Harvey directly in the eye.

Harvey took the red jack out of Kris's hand and eyed his companion carefully. "I believe that makes me the winner. Now, in spite of what you might think, I am a fair man and so, I'm giving you a final chance. If you want to back out, say so now and all bets are off."

Kris gazed across the table into Harvey's deep, hazel eyes. Steeling his nerve, he replied, "No, you won fair and square. So why don't you come and collect your prize."

With that, Harvey leaned across the table and planted a strong, sensuous kiss upon Kris's lips.

Pippa loved Kris dearly, but, like many of his friends, she had begun to despair of him. Throughout university, Pippa had never known Kris to have a girlfriend. She knew the reason why. So did Kris, deep down; it was just that he was reluctant to admit it, for some reason. So, after all the business of finals and graduation were over, Pippa decided that she was going to do something about it and introduce Kris to an old friend of hers, Harvey. She was fairly sure that if anyone could persuade Kris to open up and be honest about his sexuality, it was Harvey. Harvey was only a couple of years older than Pippa and Kris, but he had a knack for putting people at ease, and showing them a good time in the process; so Pippa decided to set up a meeting between the pair and see where it went. To her surprise, Kris readily agreed.

As they sat in the cocktail lounge waiting for Harvey to turn up, Kris began to grow nervous. "So, tell me a little more about Harvey, then."

"Where do I start?" Pippa rolled her eyes. "Harvey's Harvey."

"That's not exactly much help," Kris responded. "How about describing him to me, for a start."

"Well, he's about six foot two, has a rather sporty build; brown hair, hazel eyes and he's got the cutest arse you could possibly imagine," said a voice over Kris's left shoulder.

Kris turned around to find himself looking at the owner of the voice. Harvey obligingly executed a 360-degree twirl in order to show off his aforementioned cute backside. Almost unawares, Kris found himself nodding appreciatively.

"You can touch, if you want," Harvey offered.

Kris blushed.

"That's so sweet," Harvey said, planting a faint kiss on Kris's right cheek, then giving Pippa a hug.

All morning Kris had felt edgy about meeting the "famous" Harvey; and yet, now that Pippa's friend had finally arrived, his nerves had completely melted away. All he could think about was undressing the rakish Harvey, massaging that perfect arse and planting kiss after kiss upon those pert buttocks. As the thought flashed across his mind, Kris felt his cock begin to stir.

Harvey settled himself in the chair at Pippa's side and ran his eyes over Kris. "I say, Pip: where on earth have you been hiding this handsome fellow away?"

"Thanks." Kris grinned sheepishly at the compliment. In the few moments that he had spent in Harvey's company, the years of uncertainty had melted away and he finally admitted to himself what it was that he longed for.

Pippa nuzzled into Harvey's shoulder and whispered something into his ear. Harvey's eyes lit up with intrigue. He stroked his chin thoughtfully before saying to Kris, "Pippa here tells me that you've never..."

Kris shook his head.

"Really? How delicious. Tell you what: in order to break the ice, how about you come around to my place tonight for a quick bite and then a game of cards."

"I never gamble for money, I'm afraid," said Kris.

"Who said anything about money?" Harvey replied.

"So what will we play for, then?" Kris asked.

Harvey grinned. "Why, *you*, of course."

Now that the moment in question had arrived, Kris felt surprisingly calm about the whole situation. In order to demonstrate this, he responded enthusiastically to Harvey's kiss. Their lips locked together and their tongues began to explore each other's mouths. It felt sensational. Kris could have kicked himself for missing out on so many years' pleasure. Before Kris had a chance to make the next move, though, Harvey beat him to it. Kris felt Harvey's hands begin to massage his bottom through the denim. Kris closed his eyes and luxuriated in Harvey's touch.

After a few moments, Harvey whispered, "So, are you going to take those damn things off or what?"

Eager to oblige, Kris kicked his shoes off, then reached down and undid his belt. Sensing Harvey's eyes upon him, Kris flicked his belt away, unfastened the buttons on his jeans, but then paused before lowering them. He looked across at Harvey expectantly. "How about yourself? Aren't you going to join me?"

"Cheeky!" Harvey exclaimed, before adding, "I like it."

Harvey then proceeded to treat Kris to a slow, tantalizing striptease. As Harvey peeled away each item of clothing, Kris felt himself growing more and more excited, so that by the time Harvey was down to his tight-fitting briefs, Kris felt incredibly turned on. Almost instinctively, Kris snaked his right hand out toward Harvey. Harvey skipped out of his reach. "Ah-ah. First of all…" Harvey gestured at Kris, intimating that he should now reciprocate. Kris was more than happy to oblige and tore off his jeans and shirt. His cock strained impressively at the lining of his boxer shorts. As Kris went to take them off, Harvey said, "Allow me."

With that, Harvey knelt down in front of Kris, took hold of the flimsy material and lowered the boxers. Harvey gasped and then smiled at the sight of Kris's long, thick cock. Harvey shook his head. "To think you've been hiding this beauty all these years."

Kris nodded, slightly abashed.

"What a waste," Harvey said. "I think we better make up for lost time, don't you?"

"Absolutely," Kris nodded eagerly. No sooner had the word escaped his lips than he felt the tip of Harvey's tongue circumscribe the end of his cock. Harvey then licked the length of the shaft, before taking as much of Kris between his lips as he could manage. Kris groaned slightly, and his head rocked back. The sensation was utterly amazing, so much so that Kris sensed himself racing toward climax rather quickly. As if aware of this, Harvey broke away from sucking Kris in order to bestow a flurry of delicate kisses upon Kris's balls, upper thighs and lower stomach. Kris wondered if he had died and gone to heaven: Harvey's kisses were divine.

Slivers of precum had begun to spill from the end of Kris's cock, and Harvey gathered some of it with the fingertips of his right hand, then broke away from kissing Kris in order to lick the juice from his fingers. When Kris glanced down and caught sight of this, his cock gave an enormous twitch and spilt out even more of the sticky liquid. Harvey smeared this onto his fingers; then rose upon his haunches, raised his right hand and offered it to Kris.

Kris lowered his head and hungrily lapped up the offering. The slightly tangy flavor surprised him and turned him on even further. He wanted more, but not his own: he wanted to taste

Harvey. Kris reached down, took hold of Harvey's hands and pulled him up into a standing position. For a few long seconds, the pair gazed deeply into each other's eyes.

Breaking the spell, Harvey swept the cards off the table on which their game had been played, then the two men fell upon the felt cloth, locked tightly in each other's arms. For the next few minutes, the pair proceeded to kiss, stroke and play with each other. Finally, Harvey permitted Kris to take off his briefs. Harvey's impressive cock sprang free, brushing Kris's right forearm as it did so. Kris grabbed Harvey's cock and began to tug at it eagerly.

"Easy," Harvey laughed.

"Sorry," Kris said, and settled upon a much gentler rhythm. Harvey closed his eyes as Kris wanked him off. Though he had, of course, pleasured himself on many, many occasions, Kris could hardly believe how different it felt to have someone else's cock in his hand. He loved the way Harvey's prick twitched between his fingers as if it had a life of its own and was trying to break free of his grip. Wanting to control Harvey's excitement, Kris slackened his grip, allowing only the very tips of his fingers to toy with him, smearing the juice that had started to leak from the end of Harvey's cock up and down the impressive shaft.

Longing to reciprocate Harvey's earlier attentions, Kris went to maneuver himself around in order to take Harvey in his mouth. Realizing what Kris was up to, and not to be outdone, Harvey wriggled around also, so that the pair took up a sixty-nine position. Kris could hardly believe the gorgeous, glorious cock that now rested mere inches in front of his face. He was about to take it between his lips when Harvey beat him to it once again and began to lick Kris's balls. Kris gasped and his breathing became shallower. Desperate to respond, Kris's lips closed around the end of Harvey's erect cock.

Kris became lost in a world of pleasure. To be sucking upon a lovely stiff cock, while his own was locked between another man's lips, was the most intense, blissful experience of his life. Already Kris knew that he wanted to repeat it again and again and again. Every fiber of his body tingled. Shock waves of excitement pulsed through his thighs, groin, legs, stomach, fingers, arms and lips, such that it occurred to Kris that he might literally explode in ecstasy. And then he realized that he was. A telltale tingling in his balls informed him that he was only seconds away from climax. Wishing for them to come together, Kris sucked all the more eagerly upon Harvey's cock. Alas, his efforts proved to be in vain, for the next instant he felt a tremendous wave of pleasure crash through his groin as his cock filled Harvey's mouth with warm, creamy cum. Harvey stopped sucking and instead simply allowed Kris to spunk away, occasionally licking his tongue around the tip of Kris's dick in order to coax every last drop of juice out of it.

Eventually, Kris's climax eased. When it did so, he turned his attention back to Harvey's erection. Clearly, Harvey had found Kris's orgasm a turn-on, as his cock felt more rigid than ever in Kris's hands. Eager to please his new lover, Kris licked and sucked for all he was worth. As he sensed Harvey growing ever more excited, Kris cupped Harvey's balls in his hands and gently massaged them. Harvey let out a loud moan of delight that let Kris know he was on the verge of climax. Kris opened his mouth wide and took Harvey as far down his throat as he possibly could. Harvey's breathing shortened, and he began to make tiny panting noises. Kris withdrew Harvey's cock until only the very tip of it rested against his lips. Kris then kissed the end purposefully. His timing and technique were perfect, for the next second Harvey came, covering Kris's lips and chin with spunk. Kris then fastened his lips around the twitching cock and lapped up the last of Harvey's cum, finding it delicious.

When Harvey was finally spent, Kris sat up and began to wipe the spunk off his face. Quick as a flash, and with an incredibly naughty grin, Harvey sat up beside Kris and planted a long, luxuriating kiss upon Kris's lips, licking some of the cum off in the process. The pair didn't part until they heard the door to the room open. They discovered Pippa standing there holding a DVD disk and two cocktail glasses, both of which were brimful.

Harvey and Kris accepted the drinks gratefully, then Kris asked what the disk was. Pippa giggled as she presented it to him. "It's a present for you, silly."

Kris looked puzzled. "Of what?"

Pippa pointed across at the mirror on the far wall of the room. "Harvey likes to make little home movies and I often play camera-girl."

Kris looked down at the disk and comprehension suddenly dawned on him. "You mean, I...we...this is of us?"

Harvey smiled, "Just in case you ever doubt yourself again."

"Oh, don't worry," Kris replied, "I won't." And with that, he kissed Harvey once more.

Sensing Pippa was watching, Kris turned around and said to her, "How about making another one of those home movies?"

Pippa smiled and retreated out of the room, allowing Kris to turn his attention back to Harvey. "And this time, let's really give the censors something to think about."

Harvey grinned in response, then reached down and began to massage Kris's cock back to life. Kris decided that it was only fair to reciprocate, and so he toyed with Harvey in return. As their cocks brushed together, Harvey bestowed a series of light, playful kisses around the nape of Kris's neck. Working his way around to Kris's right ear, Harvey nuzzled the lobe tenderly, making Kris's cock throb. To Kris's disappointment, Harvey broke away momentarily in order to get off the table and nip across to the side cabinet. Kris was about to follow him; however, Harvey swiftly returned, armed with a condom and a tube of strawberry lube. Harvey grinned. "Do you want to do the honors, or shall I?"

Kris bit his lip as he weighed up his options, then, very deliberately, he turned around, leant forward on the table and wiggled his bum invitingly.

"You're sure?" Harvey asked.

Kris nodded. "I'm sure."

Harvey didn't need asking twice. He rolled the condom onto his stiff dick, squirted out a generous amount of lubricant onto his fingers and then smeared it around the crack of Kris's arse. Kris closed his eyes as he delighted at the touch, breathing deeply in preparation. Harvey took hold of Kris's bumcheeks and rested the tip of his cock at Kris's rear entrance. Before entering him, Harvey reached around and took hold of Kris's balls in his right hand. Gently kneading them, Harvey waited until Kris had grown fully erect before he eased himself in, inch by inch. Harvey couldn't believe how hot and tight it felt. He halted when his cock was halfway in and asked if it was okay. Kris was enjoying the sensation so much, he found it difficult to reply, but managed to nod his head in affirmation. Harvey then slowly started to build up a smooth rhythm, working a little more of his shaft into Kris with each forward thrust.

Kris had started to let out little low moans of pleasure. He tried to work out which experience he had enjoyed most—going down on Harvey or being fucked by him. Deciding that both were equally wonderful, Kris allowed himself to become lost in the moment. He was vaguely aware that Harvey's breathing was steadily becoming shallower and his strokes shorter and sharper. Sure enough, a second later, Harvey sank into him deeper than ever, letting out a deep sigh as he did so. Kris's arse tingled blissfully as he felt Harvey begin to twitch away inside him. His own cock practically begged to join in the fun. Sensing this, Harvey withdrew from Kris, then deftly spun him around and took Kris's cock in his mouth. Kris was so aroused it only took a matter of seconds for his cock to erupt. Kris cried for joy as Harvey sucked and lapped at his dick. When Kris was finally spent, the lovers collapsed on the table in each other's arms.

Harvey smiled, reached up and ran his left hand through Kris's hair. "So, still not sure?"

"What do you think?" Kris replied.

Harvey purred coquettishly and pursed his lips. "I think you should stay the night, just to make sure."

Kris grinned. "I thought you'd never ask." He was so glad that he had agreed to an evening of gambling with Harvey.

EVERYBODY'S BOY

Landon Dixon

I was sitting in the front seat of the pickup with the cowboy. We were parked in a deserted, weed-infested lot on Front Street. The morning sun was just rising from the other side of the river, big and yellow. Everything was quiet, empty, the crumbling buildings and streets still slumbering in the early light. Except for me and the cowboy—we were tugging on each other's bared, erect cocks.

"Gosh, but you're huge!" the cowboy gushed for the tenth time, his sky-blue eyes fastened on my ten-inch dong, his sunbrowned hand riding up and down the smooth, hot, pulsating length of my cock.

I smiled vacantly, my amber eyes slightly glazed, tugging back just as tight and quick on the cowboy's hard, throbbing slab of beef. The cowboy was around my age, young. He had a sun-tanned, eager face, thick blond hair curling out from under his white cowboy hat, and was dressed in a checked red shirt and blue jeans, his body tight and compact. I was wearing a tight white T-shirt and equally tight pair of blue jeans, adding to the boyish appearance of my face and body, my soft brown hair cut short.

"You're pretty well built yourself, cowboy," I purred, meaning it. I was getting paid, sure—the cowboy had made the long trek into the city on the strength of my rep—but that didn't mean I couldn't take some small measure of pleasure out of the transaction, too.

The cowboy's studly prick pulsed in my hand, as I absently and automatically used all the cock-handling techniques I'd picked up in three years of working the streets.

Yeah, you can jerk a cock with the best of them, I thought to myself: *stroke slow and sensual and full length, pull quick and frenzied and short, getting the shaft to spasm to your touch, buffing the cap so that it bloats around your swirling fingers. But it's a far cry from where you thought you'd be by now: a high-priced, luxuriously pampered call-boy working an elite clientele of maybe eight or ten wealthy men in first-class hotel suites. Or maybe the exclusive boy-toy of some superrich sugar daddy, living the high life in a paid-for penthouse apartment with seasonal trips to Europe and the Caribbean. Instead of hustling parking lot hand jobs with raw kids in battered trucks two blocks off skid row.*

The cowboy grunted and groaned, "Oh, Jesus! I'm gonna come! Yeah, I'm gonna come!"

I blinked my eyes, looked down at the cock I was jacking. It jumped in my hand, spurted. Hot semen leapt out the slit on the bulbous head, splashed against the dashboard. I milked the spouting dong sure and true, giving a wrist-twist at the top of the tug, jerking out pop-shot after pop-shot. The cowboy bucked, the pickup rocking. And my own cock spasmed and sprayed in the cowboy's clenching fist.

I'd been plying my trade so long I could turn it on and off like that, stoking up the sticky, sweaty, desperate eroticism with my own jetting orgasm. The cowboy loved it, whooping his delight, shooting it. We jerked in rhythm, pumping out passion in pressurized bursts in each other's squeezing, shifting hands.

The cowboy dug two twenties and a ten out of his shirt pocket and spilled them onto the seat, as I wiped and zipped. Semen dripped off the dashboard, down onto the scruffy floormats. I scooped up the money, stuffed it into my jeans and stepped out of the truck.

The harsh morning light hit me hard in the face, making my head spin. I staggered slightly, then recovered my balance and walked away from the pickup, heading for the Gay Cavalier and the gloryholes in back. Business would just be opening up at the low-down bar and blow-job emporium.

Yeah, you should've been a high-priced piece of ass by now, have yourself installed in a real rich setup. But here you are instead, pressed up against the graffiti-smeared wall of the middle stall in the dingy men's room in back of the Gay Cavalier; a man on the other side of the wall hungrily sucking your cock.

He'd been standing by the sinks, probably washing his hands for the sixth or seventh time: a tall, thin, dark-haired businessman squeezing in a sordid morning quickie before a busy day of moneymaking. The other stalls were empty, the bar out front quiet except for a few confirmed drunkards. The man was dressed in a pin-striped black suit, white shirt, pink tie, black leather shoes. The leather had the same rich, deep gloss as his hair; his fingernails were impeccably manicured, face and hands tanned.

But above the spicy scent of businessman's cologne was the sharp tang of sweat. And his gray eyes held more than a hint of desperation and despair behind the cockiness. There was a wife and kids at home, I suspected, casually meeting the man's plea and smiling my acceptance.

It takes all kinds, I mused, as the hundred-dollar bill slid under the stall wall. *And you take all kinds—all comers—and you give them exactly what they want. And what you want?* I'd moaned, half-fake, half-real, when I'd unzipped and hefted my cock and stuck it through the waist-high padded hole in the green metal wall, and the businessman had eagerly gobbled up my hood, excitedly submerged my shaft in heat and wetness.

And now my dampened palms squeaked against the wall, my breath fogging the scrawled metal, as Mr. Businessman sucked hard and tight, amateurishly but enthusiastically, trying to keep consuming all of my meat as it swelled out to its full, erect length. Impossible. My mushroomed cap hit the back of his throat and pushed the dandy back, the shaft as long and stiff as it'd been in the cowboy's hand. I had the gift of stamina and the curse. Businessman gagged and gasped and gave up the fight for all of my cock.

He blew me as best he could, his love of man-meat, which even family ties and high-society business connections couldn't break, urging him on. He sucked sloppily and jerkily. I listened to the hissing breath steaming out of his flared nostrils on the other side of the thin wall, the gurgling in his throat, feeling his frantic sucking on my cock right down to my balls.

All in a day's work. Getting blown by some stranger in a shabby downtown bar, a gloryhole hummer minus the glory. I gently pumped my hips, nonetheless, helping Businessman get a better vaccing rhythm going on my dong. *Turning fifty-dollar tricks in broken-down pickup trucks with fumbling boys, hundred-dollar suck-offs in stinking bathroom stalls with slumming businessmen—this is your typical day?* It wasn't how

I'd envisioned it at all, when I'd first started selling my cock on the street.

Businessman caught on to the pumping pace with his mouth, easing back on his greedy nature and taking what he was given, sucking smoother, tighter, more sure and sensuously. I felt the improvement, the wet, warm, wonderful sensation of velvety man-mouth tugging on my organ, and I pumped faster and more urgently.

Businessman rubbed the wall with delight, overjoyed with his cocksucking, overwhelmed with all the meaty manhood he was sucking on; his inner homo set free. I kissed the metal, squirmed my tongue over it, hands splayed out and body flattened against it, hips thrusting, cock feeding into the hungry, happy mouth on the other side.

Businessman's time was up. He'd gotten more than his money's worth. I pumped fast and furious into his mouth, then gushed down his throat, giving out a deserved bonus in salty, quivering bursts. The man swallowed with a skilled gusto born of the highly sexed situation, our mutual connection, gulping everything I gave him as I clawed at the wall in ecstasy.

The fuck-pads were on the fifth floor of the Hotel Sinclair. That's where I headed next, after leaving Businessman smacking his lips on the other side of the heated gloryhole. I thought about having a drink or two at the bar, but I knew the hot sun and clear blue sky, and the sight of the sparkling green river water would do more to clear my fuzzy head.

The Hotel Sinclair was three blocks over on Perth Avenue. The streets and sidewalks were crowded now. I was just another faceless, nameless person pushing his way through the throng, a workaday stiff in more ways than one.

You could've had it so easy, I thought to myself, as I was jostled this way and that. *Up at noon, fresh from a sound sleep between silk sheets, brunch out on the balcony, looking down on these very same masses hustling to make a buck. No worries about this month's rent, next week's food, clothing bills and transportation. You just had to grin and bear it and suck it and fuck it, treat the one man—or maybe a few on a string—right and everything would be laid out for you. No running with the little people.*

It was hot now, the sun blazing down, baking the dusty city core. It was only slightly cooler in the Hotel Sinclair and even dustier. Three old men were slumped in the musty armchairs in the dilapidated lobby. The hunchback behind the front desk glanced up only briefly from his porn mag, nodded at me, then went back to his drooling, as I thumbed the rickety elevator open and stepped inside.

The fuck-pads were quiet, empty, except for Room 512: my room. I could hear the telltale grunting and groaning even before I pushed open the door. Two men were inside: a large, muscular black man and an even larger, more muscular Hispanic. The black man sported a shaved head and body, gold earrings. His ebony muscles gleamed and bulged as he crouched down and drove his cock into the muscular ass of the man on all fours on the floor.

The Hispanic man taking the licorice dong deep into his anus had slick black hair and a slick black mustache, diamond studs in his earlobes and tattoos all over his massive, caramel-colored body. His hard buttocks rippled and his body rocked to the pounding beat of the cock reaming his ass.

The men kept right on fucking, as I walked into the room.

It was a small, narrow room, even with the bed taken out. There were a couple of mattresses thrown down on the thread-bare gray carpet; one small, round, wooden table and a couple of wooden chairs. The walls were gray and ragged as the carpet. The entire floor smelled of stale sweat and sperm. I breathed in the atmosphere, gazing at the big muscle-studs joined cock to ass, and my own cock stirred in my tight jeans. I thought, *Welcome home.*

"Tyrese," the black man said by way of unnecessary introduction. "That's Diaz." He nodded at the man on his hands and knees in front of him.

Diaz stared at my crotch with his pale-green eyes. "You're 'Little' Jason, huh?"

I nodded, as Tyrese pulled his cock out of Diaz's gulping ass and rose to his feet. Diaz got up off the floor, and the two giants towered over me, grinning, their long, hard, glistening cocks twitching up in the air.

I looked from one man to the other, one hard-on to the other, and at the squalid surroundings; thinking, *So this is your life? Wandering from truck to toilet to fuck-pad. Taking it up the ass raw and ruthless from two over-pumped musclemen in a shabby room where no one could hear you scream? Is this the best you can do?*

My cock swelled in my jeans, as I looked from the two naked studs in front of me to the two hundred-dollar bills lying on the wooden table. I pulled my T-shirt up and off, popped my jeans open and shoved them down. The bodybuilders' eyes lit up when my cock sprang out and up, surging huge and throbbing right in front of all three of us.

Tyrese and Diaz spun around and dropped down to the floor, onto their hands and knees. They arched their muscled backs, thrust out their tight-packed, mounded buttocks. I stepped out of my jeans, only slightly surprised. I'd expected them to plug and plow me between them like a fuck-toy, yes, but I'd banged big bottoms before, too. A lot of pumped-up men craved nothing more than to be pumped themselves—the bigger the cock punishing them and taking command of their asses, the better.

I picked the tube of lube up off the floor and slathered my jutting cock in slipperiness. Then I smacked Diaz's upraised buttocks, and then Tyrese's buttcheeks, with my gleaming dong. Both men grunted and quivered, asses rippling with excitement and anticipation, cocks spearing out from their loins.

I slammed my cap in between Tyrese's cheeks, up against his black manhole. My hood squished inside, and I surged forward with shaft. I didn't stop until my shaven balls kissed up against the man's backside, my entire dong buried in his hot, gripping chute.

"Fuck! Yes!" Tyrese cried, paddling a couple of hand-prints forward on the carpet with the force and fill of my cock stretching his anus.

I gripped his tight, tiny waist and pumped my hips, moving my cock back and forth inside him. I quickly torqued up the fucking pressure, stroking faster, stuffing harder, deep as I could go. I rocked the big man to and fro on his hands and knees, his muscles clenching all over his giant body. Then I abruptly pulled back and out, and plunged into Diaz's waiting ass.

The other muscleman's anus was just as tight, just as hot. I plowed through ring and drove into chute, giving Diaz just what he so badly wanted.

I was on fire, the heat of the hunky men's bodies and asses flaming my passion, driving my performance. At eleven o'clock in the morning, in a skuzzy hotel, fucking two anonymous men in the ass in a dirty room, for profit.

I grinned, drilling into Tyrese's rectum again. *Who wants to be tied down to one old man, or a group of jealous men, jacking and sucking and fucking the same old same old, day after day and night after night—a peacock in a gilded cage?*

I pulled out of Tyrese and plunged back into Diaz, pistoning that man's anus with my pipe. I had a college fraternity initiation party in the park down the block at noon—young, pretty men with young, anxious, pretty mouths and cocks and bodies excited to pay me to participate in their perverted games behind a screen of bushes. And the cop on the beat: he was scheduled for a back-alley suck and fuck early that night.

I eagerly reamed one muscleman, then the other, rejoicing in their gyrating asses and cries of pounded-out passion, reveling in my wickedly satisfying life. They jerked out their own orgasms in sizzling strips all over the floor. I tilted my head back and roared, blasting half my orgasm into Diaz's trembling ass, then uncorking my spurting hose and plugging it back into Tyrese's shuddering butt, searing the man's bowels with my sprays of utter bliss.

Is this what you always wanted? Is this as far as you're going? Leading with your cock, fucking all the time, anywhere, any men, coming and coming and coming?

Sure it is!

THE PIÑATA CONQUEST

Boot LS

I hear the rope groaning under my weight, but I don't feel any real strain. I've been hanging here for almost twenty minutes. Still have feeling in my extremities. No real pain. Actually, it's pretty nice. The strain on my joints is minimal, better than when I'm standing up. It's easier to breathe up here. I'd stay here forever if I could.

But I can't. I may not feel it, but being suspended too long can be dangerous. So one way or another, I can only stay up so long.

"Are you comfortable?" he asks, giving me a gentle nudge. I turn around slowly. He smiles at me.

"It's nice," I say, nodding as much as the ropes will allow.

"Good." He stops my twirl, kisses me. His hands in my hair, rubbing against my beard, tracing the line of my jaw. "Because it's going to get worse."

I smile. I knew that was coming. Jake never puts me up like this without a good reason. There's always a catch. Always a game.

"What are we playing?"

He smiles and steps back, lets me admire his bare chest and the lines he works so hard to keep there. I could teach an anatomy lesson with that body. At least, as far as the muscular system goes. "Piñata," he says.

Then he wheels out the table. The wheels screech and whine as it moves into my field of vision. Across the table is a pool noodle, a flogger—a leather cat-o'-nine-tails, only with three or four times more tails—what looks like a padded sword, a Wiffle ball bat, a piece of plastic piping and a strand of bamboo.

"The other guys will be here in a few minutes," he says. "Once they get here, we're going to play piñata."

I swallow, afraid I already know the answer to the question. "And how does piñata work?"

He reaches under the table and picks up a plastic bag. Inside the bag is a bunch of candy. Looks like miniatures, like the kind of candy we usually hand out to the kids in the neighborhood at Halloween.

"You put this in your mouth," he says. "And you hold it as long as you can. When you've had enough, you just have to let go."

"So that's the safeword?"

He shrugs. "Makes it pretty obvious, doesn't it?" He smiles, that charming smile that melts me a little bit on the inside. "Now, we're going to start here," he points over at the pool noodle, just a long strip of hollow foam. "And every five minutes, we're going to switch to the next toy." He picks up the bamboo. "I really hope you don't last long enough for this one," he says. "I'd hate to see the marks it would leave."

I smile at him. "So I just hold out as long as possible. Doesn't sound like that big of a deal." There's more. There always is. "What's the catch?"

He smiles and puts a blindfold over my eyes, kisses me again.

"The catch is that when you let go, you go home with whoever hit you last. Now, it's just for one night, but that's the deal."

We've talked about this. While generally monogamous, we both love the fantasy of being traded, sold like meat. Well, I love the fantasy of being sold. He likes the fantasy of selling. Of betting on who gets to use my body.

I know the guys he's invited. It has to be Larry and Brad. They're the only ones we know who we would trust to do this. They're the only ones who we know can handle it. And they're the only ones we've ever talked to about this idea. At least, the only ones we talked to seriously.

So one of them might take me home tonight. One of them might find out just how talented my tongue can be. One of them might get to use me a lot rougher than he usually uses a partner, because he'll know what I can take. They know my safewords, they know my fetishes. They know the things I like that Jake doesn't like.

And then there're the things Jake likes that I don't. Things that I normally wouldn't do, but that I will tonight. Things he knows I'll do if he wins.

I laugh. "It's going to be an interesting night," I say.

"Yes, it is." He reaches underneath and gives me some gentle attention while we wait for Brad and Larry.

I've almost cum when the knock sounds on the door. I don't think that's an accident. I don't think Jake is surprised, or disappointed, to leave me so close to the edge. Maybe I'm imagining the chuckle under his breath. But I doubt it.

"Open," he says. I open my mouth, and he puts the top of the plastic bag in. I bite down. I can breathe without difficulty. All I have to do is hold my jaw together. Clamp my teeth.

One way or another, this is all going to be over in the next half hour.

"So here's how it works," Jake says, once our guests have been shown in. "First we hit with the noodles. When the bell dings, we move to the next toy, then the next. Whoever knocks the piñata open wins the prize. And everyone knows the prize, right?"

"I'm looking forward to it," Larry says. His voice is deep. He's a smoker.

But Brad. Brad is the smart one. The clever one. The cruel one. "Why is he blindfolded?"

Actually, that's a good question. Why *am* I being blindfolded? Maybe it's so I can't throw the game, can't make sure to let go when Jake is swinging. But no. Not my Jake. There's more. There's always more.

He laughs. "Once the piñata falls, it has to guess who knocked it open. One guess. A thirty-three percent chance to guess who gave the last hit."

"And if he's right?"

Jack chuckles. "If he's right, he gets to come home in the morning. If he's wrong, then the winner gets to keep him for twenty-four hours."

Still a one in three chance of staying here with Jake. A one in three chance of just staying home, of a full day with all of the things that Jake likes to do but I don't.

I'm honestly not sure who I'm rooting for.

"Won't he just be able to count whose turn it is?" Brad says. "Doesn't matter what order we go in, he just has to follow the hits, keep track of the count, and he'll at least have good odds of knowing who gets to hit."

That's true. But I bet Jake thought of that.

"There's enough tools here for us each to have one," Jake says. "You just hit whenever you feel like it. Hit twice in a row if you want. Hit and then move. Don't hit for five minutes. Remember, the goal is not only to be the one to knock the piñata down, but also to have him guess that it was someone else."

They chuckle, and I adjust myself, steeling for the first round. The bell rings, and the first hits come in almost immediately.

Using swimming-pool noodles for beating is brilliant. They don't hurt really. There's a dull thud. But they make a lot of noise. The noise those things make is enough to make others wince. You can swing them as hard as you want, but it never makes more pain than a dull thud.

Jake knew what he was doing picking those. There's a slight sting, but for the most part all it'll do is tire them all out. As bad as the noise makes it sound, they could pound on me all day with those things, and the biggest danger I'd be in would be fear of boredom.

The one thing the noodles do manage to do is make my skin more sensitive. Which means, when the bell rings a second time, and the first hit from the flogger comes, I can feel it a bit more directly than I might have otherwise.

This time around, the hits are a bit more scattered. I think I recognize Jake's hand, the way he jerks back just a little bit at the end, the twitch that adds some sting to the thud of a flogger. Then come two quick hits, solid pounds of weight that crash into my sides.

I grunt, for the first time, and I hear snickers of satisfaction. I tighten my jaw and try to steady my breathing. Another hit comes from the other direction, almost making me gasp at the surprise instead of the pain.

"Almost had him!" Larry says.

"And if you had, he would have known it was you," Jake says.

Two hits later, Jake steps in front of me and runs his hand gently down my cheek. "It's okay," he says. "I just need to check. Can you open your mouth?"

I nod.

He laughs. "Not a trick, love," he says. "This doesn't count as being broken. I just want you to open your mouth for a second, so I can see that you can. Then we'll put the bag back in and the game will be on again."

I open my mouth, give it a stretch and then close it again on the plastic bag.

And just as I do, the bell rings. I smirk. If I didn't have something in my mouth, I'd yell at Jake for claiming that there were no tricks.

Round three starts with a solid hit to my ribs. It feels like one of the pool noodles, but with a pipe, a plastic pipe, on the inside. Same loud noise, but with a whole lot more pressure behind it, a more intense impact. The first hit makes me ache, makes me swing back and forth a little. I squeeze my hands, clench my jaw and try to pull in breaths that just won't come.

At the apex of the swing comes another hit, sending me the other direction. I clench my eyes under my blindfold, bite down and cough at the hit.

Then there's an upswing, a single hit between my legs. One solid blast, and the candy crashes to the floor. I cough, gasp for breath. I nearly vomit from the pain.

On the one hand, I'm happy it ended when it did. I don't want to know what the Wiffle ball bats would have felt like. I certainly don't want to know what the bare piping or the bamboo would have done to me.

I am a bit surprised it took that long to hit between my legs, actually. I'm not complaining, but I expected them to think of it sooner.

Jake pulls the blindfold off my eyes and rubs my jaw, kisses away the tears. After a few seconds, when I can breathe again, he kisses me gently. Then he helps turn me toward the others.

"Okay," he says. "Time to guess. Who took the last hit?"

I take a deep breath and look at the guys. Jake stands with his arms crossed, barely breathing hard, smiling and sweating a little. He locks eyes with me, the view of a sinner and a saint, but mostly a sinner.

Brad smiles, nervous. He won't make eye contact with me.

Larry also won't look at me, but he looks bored. Like it all comes down to a foregone conclusion. Like he not only knows who hit me, he knows who I will choose. Like he's not surprised.

Why wouldn't he be surprised? Why won't Brad make eye contact?

Maybe Brad won't make eye contact because he feels bad about it. Maybe he's guilty for hitting me there. And that guilt is written so clearly on his face that Larry doesn't feel like there's any chance I'll pick him. And Larry knows that since *he* didn't deliver the final hit, he doesn't get me anyway.

Unless it's a bluff. Maybe he wants me to think that he doesn't care, wants me to guess someone else, so that he'll get the full twenty-four hours.

But then, why would Brad be so guilty looking? Why would he avoid my gaze?

I look over at Jake, but he is no help. He smiles, knowing that it truly *doesn't* matter what I choose. At best, he gets twenty-four hours of pushing my soft limits. At worst, he gets to have that experience of trading me away, and I come back in one day. We talk about it, we decide if we want to do it again and we have fantastic sex.

If it was Jake, and I guess him, then I don't have to worry about what he'll do as much, because it won't be as long.

But then, if it was him, he'll find some other way to get past the soft limits. He'll have plenty of chances for that. Tonight wasn't about that. It wasn't about Jake getting to do extra things. It was about us experimenting with this fantasy.

Which means it has to be one of the others.

Fifty-fifty. Guess right, and I go home with one of them for the night. Guess wrong, and it's twenty-four hours.

I smile at Jake. "Are you sure?" I ask him. "It's not too late to back out. Not too late to change our minds."

Jake smiles. "It's okay," he says. "Just guess."

I look over at Brad and Larry. Brad is guilty. Larry is confident.

I sigh. "I think it's going to end up with twenty-four hours," I say. "With Larry."

BIG THICK DICK AND DOUBLE-CHOCOLATE BUBBLE BOOTY

Shane Allison

I notice this beefy-looking tall brotha walk in. I've seen him before. I fucked him once in a bookstore bathroom. He's quiet and has dick for days. I think he works at some motel; I don't know. I follow him into the back of the dirty bookstore. Damn, look at the ass on him! A double-chocolate bubble booty I could eat off of for days and still have leftovers. I bet he looks delicious naked. He sees me but pretends I'm not there. He walks into one of the booths in the far corner of the back. I twist the doorknob in hopes that it's open. It's not. I hear money being worked into the machine. I hear the *ohs* and *ahs* of a woman being fucked. I hear the slurps of a dick being sucked. I tap gently on the door. I know he can hear me. He knows it's me. I wish he would let me in. I really want to suck his dick. I want to smash my face between the double-chocolate bubble cheeks of his booty. I hate when guys play hard to get. The *ohs* and *ahs* are enough to make my dick hard. I bet he's got his dick out. Damn, I wish he would let me in. I want to see his dick. I want to drop to my knees and put his dick in my mouth. I would suck him so good. I would give him the best blow job ever. I want him to sit his double-chocolate ass on my face. I want his dick to kiss the back of my throat.

I'm so fucking horny right now. I hate hard-to-get guys. I circle the back like a dick-hungry shark. The gay porn DVDs locked behind the plate glass make my dick crazy-hard. Damn, look at the dicks on these guys! They've got some big nice asses, too. I love rimming a nice juicy ass. This place is cleaner than where I usually go. They have better gay porn movies, and it doesn't smell like piss. This place isn't run by gay-hating girls armed with flashlights, yelling at you to get in a booth. Bitches! They only have guys working here. Some of them are really cute. There's one guy who works here I would love to fuck. He's tall, a little on the heavy side. I bet he looks good naked and has a bodacious ass. This place is convenient for me because it's on my way home. Yeah, this place kicks the ass of the place I usually go. I'm sick of seeing the same guys whose dicks I have sucked over and over.

Someone new just walked in. He's cute, slightly older than Double-Chocolate Bubble Booty. He looks to be in his early forties, Native American–looking, though I'm not sure. He's wearing a white T-shirt, painter pants with paint stains on them and dusty tan boots. He looks familiar. I watch him take one of the booths in the corner. He looks at me like he wants me. I'm grabbing at my dick. He watches me grab at my dick. I walk over where his door is cracked open. He unzips his painter pants and takes out his dick. He hikes his T-shirt up over his belly. I see dark waves of hair on his stomach. He puts in some money. Someone is getting fucked. Someone is getting his dick sucked, from what I can hear. I'm so fucking hard right now. I need to suck some dick. I wedge the door open enough to slide in between him and the small bench in his booth. Our bellies rub together. This is meant to be. Straight porn plays out on the TV. I waste no time. I sit down on the bench and put his dick in my mouth. It's soft, yeah, but it doesn't take long to get hard. Jesus, his dick is huge. Wait a minute, I know this guy. I knew he looked familiar. I've sucked his dick before at the other place. I've had him in one of the booths at the other place, where they don't have good gay porn movies, where it always smells like cum.

I remember him saying, "Make that dick come! Make that dick come!" He came all over my shirt that night. He had a lot of cum built up. Now it's like his dick won't stop growing in my mouth. I suck him slow. I've got my lips tight around his dick. I love sucking dick. I could suck dick all day. I would take load after load down my slutty fucking throat. He's moaning. He likes the way I'm sucking his dick. I can tell. It's one of the biggest I've had in my mouth. I mean he's gotta be like nine inches, six inches around. Gimme this dick! Nice and fucking juicy. I grab ahold of his hips. I push in. He shoves it all the way back in my throat. I didn't know I could take a dick this size so deep. I shut my eyes. I need to focus on all this meat I'm getting.

Slurp. Slurp. Slurp.

I take it all the way. I've worked up a thick mix of spit. Big Thick Dick stands up on top of the bench over me. His dick is point blank to my face. I put it back in my mouth. Yeah, I'm gonna make this dick come. Big Thick Dick grabs my head, mashing me on his dick. It stretches my throat. I don't gag. Big Thick Dick reaches over my shoulder and unlocks the door to the booth. He cracks it open just a little. He wants someone to see us, to see me sucking his humongous dick. It's cool. I don't mind. Big Thick Dick wants someone to watch him give my slutty throat a beating.

Slurp. Slurp. Slurp.

I'm turned on to the thought of someone walking in on us. I want someone to watch me suck this guy off. Big Thick Dick grabs me, holding my throat on his dick. I want to worship him on the regular. My throat would be good and stretched. My spit leaks around his dick. Drool trickles down my chin and shirt. Fuck yeah! I'm getting my mouth used. He pulls out suddenly. *Dude, what the fuck?* I'm hungry for him. We move out in the back. I sit my naked, bare ass on the cold gray linoleum floor. I open up. He shoves his dick back into my mouth. Someone's going to see us. We're going to get caught. My heart beats fast at the thought of being seen. Big Thick Dick tells me that my mouth is wet just like a pussy. I take my glasses and tuck them into my breast pocket. I hold on to the backs of his thighs. I tighten my lips like a rope. I'm gonna make him come. He slides all the way to the back. *Deep-throat that dick!* I'm such a slut!

Someone is standing there watching me get my throat used. It's Double-Chocolate Bubble Booty. I sense him getting closer. He unzips his jeans and pulls out his double-chocolate dick. I gotta have him.

"Let him suck you," Big Thick Dick says to Double-Chocolate Bubble Booty. I have two big ole dicks in my face now and switch off sucking them both. Fuck yeah; I'm servicing two sweet dicks. This is so fucking hot! I'm so glad I came here. I work my dick stiff in my hands as Big Thick Dick and Double-Chocolate Bubble Booty take turns using my whorish mouth. I gag, but they don't give a shit. They just want to get their nuts off. I love being used like this. Both of them are going to come so hard. I can tell.

"Suck that dick," Big Thick Dick says. Double-Chocolate Bubble Booty just stands there with his dick in my mouth. I'm sucking him good. This isn't the only time I have had the chance to suck two dicks. Fuck, this is so hot! Double-Chocolate Bubble Booty whispers that he's gonna come. I suck him harder and harder. My lips are good and tight around his dick. I'm showing these men that I know how to take a dick. He comes. Double-Chocolate Bubble Booty fills my mouth. I throat his load like the cum-slut I am. He comes a huge load. He pulls out and shoots what's left on my face. I lick Double-Chocolate Bubble Booty's cum from my dick-sucking lips. Fuck yeah!

Big Thick Dick yanks my head to his piece. "Me next," he says. I open my mouth as wide as humanly possible. I relax all my muscles except my throat. Big Thick Dick is fucking my mouth hard. I'm all teary-eyed as he smashes his dick against my throat. Double-Chocolate Bubble Booty has zipped up and left. I know I will see him again. He knows now how much I love sucking a nice dick. Big Thick Dick pushes my head in. He holds his dick there until something comes. I can taste his juices tumbling down my dick-sucker throat. I grip his hairy bubble painter butt as he fills me, as he feeds me his cum. A string of his juice hangs from the tip of his dick to my lips. He works his dick back into his boxers and zips up his painter pants. I sit there half-ass naked, cum-drool running down my chin onto my work shirt. The loads of Double-Chocolate Bubble Booty and Big Thick Dick are still thick in my throat. Mmm...nice!

Big Thick Dick takes a Kleenex and jots something on the tissue. He hands it to me. It's a cell-phone number. "You're the cock-sucking slut I've been looking for," he says, and walks off. I pull up my pants and get up off the floor. I wipe my mouth clear of cum-drool with my sleeve. I pluck a few tissues out of a box and wipe the sweat off my face. I take a few deep swallows in an attempt to wash down all the cum I've just throated. I put my glasses back on and pocket Big Thick Dick's number. I know I will call him. I wouldn't mind a big Twinkie-size dick like that stretching my throat a few days out of the week.

I spend the next several hours sucking the dicks of a few geezers, but I don't let them come in my mouth. I can't get enough. I have let about eight guys use my throat so far tonight, and it's only nine o'clock.

CASE CLOSED

K. Lynn

Joe shifted in the passenger seat of the squad car, watching the tall office buildings pass as they drove by. He counted himself lucky that their pace was actually in the normal range today, since his partner Frank tended to lean heavily on the gas pedal whether they were going to a call or just going to lunch. The one time Joe complained about it, reminding Frank that nonemergency situations didn't warrant breaking the speed limit, his partner had looked at him and said, "Kid, everything's an emergency situation, as far as I'm concerned."

He turned to look at his partner, whose hands gripped the steering wheel tight. Despite Frank being twenty years his senior, the seasoned cop didn't look like his body had accrued the forty-five years he claimed. With firm muscles and a solid body, Frank could chase down most suspects and not even break a sweat. Frank and Joe would often challenge each other at the gym, seeing how much they could each bench-press, but Frank always won. Being young wasn't such an advantage when your partner held the department record for weight lifting.

On the upside, Joe's youth hadn't been an issue for Frank, as he had feared. Joe had heard horror stories of young recruits getting paired up with old, burnt-out beat cops and regretting their choice to enter the Academy. But that hadn't happened with Frank. One year together and they had meshed so well that they were getting commendations for their work. It was a dream come true for Joe. He knew that this was going to be a solid foundation for him to ascend the ranks of the police force. But that was far in the future. For now, he was happy and settled with Frank.

Well, happy enough. Because as much as he loved hanging out with the man, trading stories and sharing meals, there was also a strong pull of want in Joe's gut. His partner was a walking wet dream, and Joe had spent many nights jerking off to the mental image, but he'd be damned if he'd share that bit of information with Frank. Bad enough he was gay, but lusting after his partner made it worse. He just had to keep his desires in check and it would be okay. It had worked so far.

No one on the force was out. He learned early on in his training that he should keep his mouth shut and just do his job. Joe wasn't saying the force was homophobic, but it was better to be able to trust the guys had your back than wonder if they were going to stab you in it. Frank was no exception. His partner didn't ever come out and announce he was straight, but the long line of women he left in his wake was a strong indication that he wasn't playing on Joe's side of the fence. So, Joe just kept his fantasies under wraps and pretended it was all good.

Joe had gotten so lost in his thoughts that he was slow to realize their surroundings had changed. Instead of the brushed steel exteriors of downtown, the edges of the road were dotted with rundown buildings that had long since been abandoned.

Joe recognized the area, the middle ground between the business district and the warehouse district near the docks. Not that there was any money there either, as the shipping industry had been hard hit by the recession. It seemed like the area they patrolled was growing less populated and he wondered if, before long, the city itself would be the only place that saw action.

"Where are we headed?" Joe asked, looking over to Frank.

"Warehouse down by the river," his partner said, jutting his chin toward the windshield. "Got something that needs checking out."

Joe tried to remember any calls that had come in for them, or any open cases that might take them outside their normal patrol area, but he was coming up empty.

"I didn't hear the radio."

Frank laughed, glancing at him and then back to the road. "You've been so inside your head this morning, I'm surprised you heard anything."

"I've just got a lot on my mind," Joe said, trying to be subtle as he readjusted his position. "But I don't remember any open cases around here. And I've been with you the whole time, so what's up?"

"Just something that came through when you were grabbing us breakfast. I figured we could head by sometime and play out my hunch. It's probably nothing." He dropped his speed a little, turning the corner. "Besides, we haven't got anything else going on, and I wanted a change of scenery."

"You couldn't have picked a nicer area to go sightseeing?" Joe asked, wrinkling his nose as the faint odor of fish ran through the vents. "It smells like a filthy aquarium."

"You're too damn picky, I ever tell you that?" Frank asked, but his tone made it clear he was joking. "Won't eat at the Mexican place on Fifth, don't want to go running with me in the morning and now you're bitching about a little fish smell."

"Funny how all those things are a threat to my general health," he said, taking a closer look at the building they were pulling up to. It looked like someone had taken about twenty spray cans to it, angry words overlapping one another and vying for attention. "Are you sure this is safe?"

Frank just rolled his eyes, shaking his head as he took the key out of the ignition and opened his door. "Don't worry, princess. I'll protect you."

Joe just thinned his lips, not saying another word. He followed Frank into the warehouse, staying at the ready in case he needed to pull his weapon. Joe wasn't sure if someone or something might jump out at him, and he didn't want to take any chances.

"Ease up," Frank said, nodding down at Joe's gun. "There's nothing in here that needs that."

"Yeah, well, I'd rather not take my chances."

Frank shrugged. "Suit yourself. I'm going to go check out the back. Stay here and stand guard."

Joe watched Frank walk away, then round a corner to disappear behind a row of packing crates. He turned back toward the front, looking over the mess scattered across the floor. Discarded paper cups, a bundle of rope and some bent nails were the only thing left from whatever escape the last occupants had made. If Joe had to guess, going by the fine layer of dust that coated everything, the building had stood empty for a while. He wondered what kind of hunch Frank had had that would take them out to an abandoned warehouse. Joe certainly couldn't see any kind of clues that would signal this was the key to any case.

He walked closer to the wall, checking out the pipes that ran overhead. Like the rest of the place, they were dirty, and Joe could see a bit of rust on certain spots. He tapped at the one closest to him, coughing as a layer of dust filtered down on his head. Joe wished Frank would hurry up so they could get out of here.

Hearing a noise over his left shoulder, he started to turn around, but was caught from behind and had his arms pinned to the side. Joe fought against his attacker, kicking out and trying to free himself, but the grip just got tighter.

"Let me go. I'm a cop," he said, twisting his body to no avail.

"Shh," a voice whispered in his ear. "Calm down."

Joe recognized that voice, since he heard it beside him every day. The fight left his body. "Frank? What the hell are you doing?"

"You'll see," Frank said, loosening his hold on Joe and stepping back.

Joe turned around, taking in the sight of his partner. Frank's posture was stiff, tension evident in his muscles. "What's going on?"

"Strip," Frank said, his voice even.

Joe gave a laugh. "What? Frank, we don't have time for jokes today." He started to move, but Frank blocked his way and grabbed hold of Joe's arms, pressing his fingers into the younger man's flesh.

"I said strip," he said again. His expression had grown cold, no hint of the happy guy that had been there just five minutes before. Frank released his grip on Joe and stepped back. "Don't make me ask again."

Joe could tell his partner wasn't joking. He stood still for a moment, just watching this man who he thought he knew. With an unsteady hand, he reached up to the top button on his shirt and started undoing it, working his way down until he was at his waistband.

"While I appreciate the slow striptease, I'd advise you to work faster," Frank said. "Or else you're going to start making me angry."

Joe took the hint and quickened his actions. He pulled his shirt out of his waistband, unbuttoning the last two buttons and discarding the outer garment on the dusty floor. He grabbed the edges of his white T-shirt, pulling it up and over his head, tossing it to the side as well.

"Looking good," Frank said, nodding. If Joe wasn't mistaken, he could see a hint of lust in the older man's eyes. What the hell was going on? "Now the rest."

Joe bent over and unlaced his shoes, then stood up and toed them both off. Next he unfastened his buckle and pants, the weight of his duty belt threatening to pull down the material on its own. He pushed everything down his legs, then stepped out of it so that he was just standing there in his socks and boxer shorts. The air was slightly cool without anything to cover him and he could feel goose bumps starting to rise on his arms.

Frank reached back with one hand, pulling his handcuffs off his belt. "Turn around and put your hands up. Thread these over the pipe to lock yourself in."

"Seriously, Joe, this is going too far," he said, trying to buy himself some time. He didn't know what was going to happen, but he got the feeling he wasn't going to like it.

"Take them and do as I said," Frank said, shaking the cuffs at him.

Joe reached out, flinching as his hot skin touched the cool metal. He turned to look at the wall, the only view he was going to have until this was over. Joe locked the cuff around his left wrist, then brought both his hands up so they were touching the pipe. He had to stretch in order to grab the cuff with his right hand, then work it so that he could lock it with his left. Once he was done, he let his body relax down, grunting as the edge of the metal dug into the bottom of his palms. He had no time to concentrate on that, though, as he felt Frank come up behind him, crowding against his back and pressing his crotch against Joe's ass.

"You thought your secret was safe, huh?" Frank asked, leaning to whisper in Joe's ear. "But you forget, I'm a damn fine cop. I could sniff you out the first time I saw you. Lusting after me, probably thinking about me so you can get hard every night." Frank pushed up against him, reaching around to cup Joe's half-hard cock. "Look at you, already begging for it. All your dreams coming true."

"Frank, please," Joe moaned as Frank squeezed at his cock. "Why are you doing this?"

"Because I can," Frank said, trailing his hand up to the waistband of Joe's boxers. "And because you want it."

"I'm sorry," Joe said, his voice cracking. "I didn't mean to. And I've got a handle on it, I promise."

Frank stilled his hand where it was playing along the line where Joe's skin met elastic. "You think I'm mad about this?" He whispered in Joe's ear once again. "I'm not mad. I'm ecstatic."

Joe froze at the admission. What? This made no sense. Frank was straight. Wasn't he? "You are?" he asked, his heart pounding.

"Of course I am. Why should I risk my neck finding some fine piece of ass every few weeks when I have you ready to give it up whenever I want?" He stepped back and grabbed Joe's boxers, yanking them down so that they pooled at his feet. "I'll just have to teach you the error of your ways."

Joe couldn't speak; he really couldn't deny what Frank was saying. His partner was a lot more observant than Joe had given him credit for. But what did he expect? He stood still, just listening to the sounds coming from behind him. Joe could hear Frank fumbling, his duty belt clanging as he moved. He heard a snap, then a clatter as Frank threw something on the floor.

"First lesson is to remind you whose cock you've been jonesin' for all this time," Frank said, slipping a finger down the cleft of Joe's ass. He could tell that his partner had slicked up the digit, though he didn't know where he had gotten the lube from. Did Frank just carry it around with him, tucked inside one of his pockets? The thought made his cock harden a little more.

"You like that?" Frank asked, touching the edge of Joe's hole and then pushing his finger inside. Joe clenched around the intrusion, but Frank just kept up his motions, pushing in and pulling out a few times before a second digit joined in to start stretching him. "You aching for it?"

"Yes," Joe said, his voice unsteady. "I want...I want you to fuck me."

Frank removed his fingers and Joe almost cried out at the loss. But he didn't have long to wait, as he soon felt Frank's hands on his hips and the tip of Frank's cock nudging between his cheeks. "Class is in session, kid," he said, and that was the only warning Joe had before Frank plunged into him, deep and hard, in one swift movement. Joe felt like he was suffocating, filled up and no room to breathe. He pulled against his restraints, the pain of the cuffs playing hard against the pleasure he was starting to feel.

Frank didn't say anything else as he fucked. He pressed his fingers into the skin of Joe's hips, holding him in place as he just grunted and worked himself in and out of Joe's body. The younger cop cried out each time Frank hit his prostate, his cock hardening to the point where it was almost painful. He needed to touch it, but he couldn't. It was all up to Frank now. He was in charge.

"Please, please," Joe begged. "Get me off."

Frank didn't answer, but instead just sped up his motions. Joe was sure there would be bruises on his hips, as hard as Frank was holding him. It seemed to take forever, the minutes passing by without him knowing how long it had been, but finally Frank seized up for an instant and was spilling inside him. His cock pulsed inside Joe's body, again and again, filling Joe with come. Joe felt Frank push inside him, deeper, once, twice, and then pull back and out, leaving Joe empty. He could feel come dripping between his asscheeks and he was sure it would leak out when he moved, but he was in too much pain to concentrate. Joe needed Frank to get him off, or at least unlock the cuffs so he could do it himself.

He closed his eyes, willing himself to stay focused. Joe didn't know how he would explain the bruises. He'd have to make sure to change in privacy until they faded.

Joe jerked away as he felt someone touch his left hand. Opening his eyes, he looked to see Frank unlocking the cuff. His partner had fastened his pants again, looking like he had just been standing around, with no evidence of what had just happened.

Once his hand was released, Joe fell to the floor, his still-cuffed right hand going straight to his cock. He grabbed hold of his erection, pumping his hand up and down its length as the cuff clanged against the floor with each stroke. He was so close that it didn't take long before he was coming, white spurts coating the dusty concrete in front of him.

He tried to get his breathing under control: it had all happened so fast, he was still trying to catch up. Joe startled when a key landed beside him, and he looked up at his partner.

"Unlock yourself."

Joe looked back down, reaching for the key with a shaky

hand. It took him three tries, but he finally got it into the lock and undid the cuff. Just as he suspected, both his wrists were lined in red and there were spots of blood where the metal had dug in.

"Hand them over," Frank said, his tone flat and revealing no emotions. Joe did as he was told, offering up the key and cuffs before hunching back into himself. "Clean yourself up. I'll be waiting in the car."

With that, Joe could hear Frank's footsteps retreating. He didn't dare look up, didn't want to see him go. When it was silent again, he pushed himself up, standing on shaky feet. Joe reached down and grabbed his boxers, pulling them up his legs again. His cock was sticky inside the material, his ass wet and sore, but he had nothing to clean himself with. Going over to where he had dropped his clothes, he began pulling them on. His uniform was dusty, and even after he beat his hands against the pants and shirt, there were still streaks he couldn't get out. But maybe he looked good enough until he could get back to the station and change uniforms.

Joe walked outside, shielding his eyes against the morning sun, and saw that Frank was sitting in the squad car. He went over, his body still unsteady, and opened the passenger door. Frank didn't look over at him when he got inside. Instead, he just turned the ignition on. Joe thought he was just going to leave without saying a word, but his partner finally broke his silence.

"You've got a lot to learn, kid. That was Lesson One." Frank shifted the car into gear and headed out, leaving Joe to wonder what Lesson Two would be.

LIGHT-RAIL

Calvin Gimpelevich

The light-rail rolled in: overcrowded, noisy, pushing forward. The doors slid open and I shoved myself on, fumbling the ticket into my pocket.

I hated public transit: trash everywhere, sketchy seats and riding ass-to-elbow with every transient in town. A kid screamed. The woman next to me jacked the volume up on her headphones and I could hear top-forty pop tinning out the little foam pads. Something scratched at my neck.

I had already taken the morning off work to get my truck in the shop—thank god I already had tools on-site—and considered staying late to make up; maybe finish the job early to help pay for my broken engine. This was the third time it had crapped out on me, and I wanted an upgrade. I was thinking bright silver, raised wheels and a new rack around the bed. Something manly, useful and flashy. Like me.

The metro jerked to a stop. Some kid lost his footing and slammed into me before rushing out into the world. I brushed myself off, stuck a hand in my pocket and realized my wallet was gone.

"Fuck." I couldn't see him in the station crowd. The doors shut and we started moving before I could get out and run the little bastard down. "Fuck me."

A woman glared. Loose floral print covered her from head to toe. I scowled and she went back to her book. I could look forward to a couple of hours wasted on the phone canceling all my cards and losing sixty bucks for a new driver's license. I'd strangle that kid if I could. I'd like to put some alligator clamps on his nipples; then pull them off and watch him squirm as the blood rushed back. See how many times I had to do that before he started begging me to let him return my shit. I would bind his wrists together and make him choke on my cock.

I like to top. Really like it. And construction work keeps me in good enough shape to dominate even the most reluctant bottoms. I started out working when I was still in high school, after school—trying to prove that a scrawny Asian kid could haul concrete—and ended up loving it. Fuck the SATs. I'd worked construction for almost fifteen years and it got me a house, a nice car and no debt. More than I could say for my college-educated peers. Now I work as a contractor, doing the detailed work on big projects. That day, I was scheduled to put in floors for some half-finished office buildings the next town over, if I could get to the damn site without anything else going wrong.

Another big stop and another mass of people jostled on. It was getting so that every standing body had to press sardine-style against his neighbor. In my case, it was a guy who'd just squeezed in next to me. We made eye contact and he held my gaze. There was a defiant playfulness in his face that made me look down. The contours of an erect penis strained against his pants.

He looked like a college student: ripped jeans, fitted shirt and shaggy blond hair that wisped over his eyes—eyes so big and blue they were almost *too* big, almost, with big Bambi lashes softening the angular face. He had a straight nose and full pink lips. He looked like it'd been a few days since his last shave, the pale stubble framing mouth and chin. He couldn't have been more than twenty. Too lean, young enough not to have finished filling out.

He was short—a head shorter than me—but lean muscles rippled across his arms as he held on for balance. The T-shirt showed hard little nipples perched atop a modest pectoral shelf. A wiry trail of hair leaked out from his sleeves. The same type of hair I suddenly imagined curling around his dick and sheathing his balls. He looked down at his crotch then back at me, daring me to inspect it.

It was big, thick and tucked along his leg, fighting the fabric of his faggy tight jeans. I smiled. He inched closer so his cock pressed into my thigh. I could have wrapped an arm around his waist. He swayed against me to the rhythm of the train. I thought about those pretty lips on my dick. It twitched.

"Dirty boy," I whispered in his ear. "Cruising on the train like a little slut."

He tilted his chin up and whispered back "What are you going to do about it?"

Exactly what I wanted to hear. I hooked my hands into the sides of his pelvis, firm enough to let him know who was in charge but subtle enough that no one else was likely to notice, and guided him around so I faced his back, then pulled his tight ass into my prick and let him feel the erection swell. He pressed back, dick-hungry.

Gently, very gently, I started to hump the college boy. I tried to keep the same look of bored indifference that most other passengers wore. Nobody could tell what was going on unless they looked at our crotches, obscured by every other commuter standing by.

I love to tease. A long painful buildup made the final fucking so much more satisfying than sticking it in the moment I got hard. Discipline: that's what made it good. Rubbing up against this kid, not knowing if I'd get the chance to finish, built the sweetest agony. I dug my fingers further into his hip bones as the wanting started to hurt.

"Almost at my stop, boy. Are you getting off?"

"I can follow you."

"Good."

We exited the train, him trailing after me like a puppy. Like a good submissive, he didn't speak. I led us to my worksite. It was lunch for most of the crew. They sat around the site, ripping into soggy ham-on-ryes and PB&Js. I knew about half of the guys from working different jobs around town. They hollered at me and fist-bumped me as I walked by. College boy kept his distance, but the blue eyes continued to follow.

I got to the scaffolding outside my building and started to climb. I motioned for him to join me. The boy better not be afraid of heights. We were on a seven-story building, and I had work on the fifth floor. If people noticed him scaling the restricted area, they didn't comment. He could have been my apprentice.

I stopped about where I'd left off yesterday and swung into the room. In a couple of months this was going to be another office building; right now it looked like slabs of concrete stacked on top of each with all the artistry of a four-year-old's Legos. Some of the inner walls had been put in and loose electrical wiring hung erratically from the ceiling.

The room smelled like sawdust. That floor, like everything above it, hadn't had the front wall installed, so metal grating and wooden beams were all that shielded us from the street outside. I could see everything happening down below, but it would make a real kink in someone's neck to try watching me. The wind blew in, shifting the dirt, screws and papers lining the unfinished floor. That, combined with the cement flooring, gave the whole thing a postapocalyptic feel. The boy looked nervous. He looked over the edge, but didn't get near. It was a long way down.

I leaned against a steel girder in the middle of the space. In a couple of weeks it would be the core of a wall dividing the giant room in two. "Did you come for the view?" I asked.

He shook his head. Grinned. "I haven't come at all, yet."

"Then get over here." He did. The crotch of his jeans was stretched so tight that walking looked painful. Looked like he needed me to stretch him out on his back and fuck him until he shot all over himself. But I wasn't feeling that charitable. I had some aggression to work out.

I pulled his chin up to my face and stuck my tongue down his throat. Warm him up for gagging on me later. He let his hands wander, grabbing my ass, sliding up my shirt, reaching down to the lump in my pants. It felt good. I pushed him down so his face was near buried in it, and unzipped.

I smiled as he stared at my cock, taking in the size of it—seven inches of cut meat, thick enough to stretch an asshole to capacity, dripping precum, so hard that it ached. I grabbed a handful of spiky, soft hair and guided his lips to the tip. He licked the head, took it into his mouth and sucked on it before swallowing the entire thing. Stubble poked at my balls. I pulled his head in closer and started to fuck his face, letting the feeling sweep over my dick. Figured he'd choke on it but the boy sucked cock like professional, opening his throat to take the entire thing, lips stretched wide as they could go.

I leaned against the girder, hips bucking against his mouth. I could have shot my load right there and watched the cream slide down that pretty face. Instead, I pushed him off, emptying his throat all at once. He gaped for a moment, like I'd taken his pacifier away. Dick-hungry.

I yanked him back up and grabbed one of the loose cords hanging down on us. None of it had been hooked up yet, so the wires were safe. He started to look nervous when I tied his wrists up above his head, but didn't complain. I liked watching him endure the discomfort. He had discipline. I respected that. I pulled his T-shirt up so it hung around his hands.

He had the torso of an underwear model: washboard abs and thick shoulders. His body hair grew thicker than expected, scattered along his chest and happy trail. It bushed out at his armpits, holding in the sweat and musk. What set him apart were the two horizontal scars running along the base of his pecs. They curved up to his armpits like anchors. I'd seen scars like that before: on marching topless boys during pride, on a go-go dancer at the club, but never this close. I ran a finger across one shiny line and watched the combative unease on his face.

I suddenly realized what kind of boy I had with me. There weren't many other clues. The height, sure, but some guys are short. I paced around him, looking closer. Not a woman, just another scruffy boy.

Standing close behind him I started to rub against his ass. Grabbed it, slapped it, and let my cock push into the denim covered crack. He moaned.

"Do you want my dick?"

"Yes."

"Yes what?"

"Yes, Sir."

"Then I'm gonna need to see yours." He didn't answer. I

unzipped his fly and pulled out a big flexible dildo carved well enough to look real. It was circumcised, complete with a pee hole, veins and peach shading to match his skin. The thing felt warm from being pressed against his body and the material gave when I touched it—as close to real as plastic gets.

I pulled the pants off. They were so tight I had to peel them off. A black leather harness held his dick in place. Sunlight glinted back from the buckles. This time I wasn't surprised. I hadn't ever fucked a transboy before, but I'd watched them and wondered. I had fucked a woman in high school. Well, I'd tried. We were drunk and I couldn't get it up, let alone in. Hadn't been curious about pussy since—but also hadn't found one on a boy.

He had a tight little ass. The hair stood out and got thicker toward his crack. I slapped one cheek, then the other, until both sides were red. I ran a finger along his taint and circled the pink asshole. I felt his hole shudder, then his entire body along with it, as I stroked the sensitive skin. I went along his taint to the bottom of his cunt but didn't go farther. Wasn't sure I wanted to deal with that. Yet. Instead, I slipped a finger in his ass. He swallowed it whole, then another and another.

There was a condom in my wallet. Such a shame. For a moment I was tempted to go bare. Self-control won out. I slid the rubber over my dick, then rubbed the head in his asscrack, waiting as long as humanly possible before shoving it in. He spasmed. Started saying "fuck" over and over again. I clamped my hands into his hip bones and used them like handles to force his ass onto my dick. I fucked him hard and fast, watching him take everything in. This time I didn't last long before unloading inside of him.

The boy didn't look even close to being done. He writhed and squirmed as I pulled out, wanting more. He hung there, wrists trapped, unable to touch himself while I took my time watching. Putting my dick back into place.

Our bodies were so different. Everything about me was thick and dark in comparison. Years of working with my body had earned me the physique I'd coveted all my life. Course black hair covered my arms, legs, chest. And my dick didn't strap off.

A jigsaw revving up nearby ripped through our quiet. Voices, loud, all business, yelling out measurements and warning one another to watch the fuck out. It sounded like lunch hour had ended. My boy was still hanging naked from the ceiling. I really hoped no one needed to come in here. Fucking on the job was generally frowned on.

I undid his hands. Angry red lines showed where the cord had dug into his skin. He rapped the circulation back in before reaching for the puddle of jeans around his ankles.

"Leave it." He dropped the denim. "I'm not finished with you." I grabbed him by the back of the neck and led him over to edge, facing the long drop down. Half a foot farther and he'd fall off the edge. There were people working down there, but no one on the scaffolding too close to us. I let my hand slide down to that other opening between his legs and slipped a finger in. Salty wet lube dripped down my hand.

He wanted more. I massaged my cock through my pants. The blood started flowing back, not hard as before, but getting there. Another finger inside and he started making noise. I reached for my fly but he stopped me.

"Wait."

"What'd you say, boy?"

"Please wait, Sir. There's another condom in my jeans, Sir."

"Fine. Bring it." He did. I ripped open the foil package and put on the snakeskin.

"Now get on your knees."

His head faced the drop. Naked, vulnerable and hot for my cock. He looked like any other boy from behind. I ran the tip of my cock through his cleft. Soft, wet, and warm. It felt good. His hips bucked down, trying to push my dick in the hole. I pushed back. Everything I had slid through the lips, running up unfamiliar parts. My hand found his dick—not the rubber extension, but his hormone-addled little boy-dick rigid with blood and wet from himself. When I hit that he moaned. Then "Oh...oh my god," as I flicked over it. His cock was the length and width of my thumb.

Every time I pulled back he contracted, the hole trying to suck me in. After a while I let him. Slowly, so slowly, I entered his cunt. It was tight. I felt him stretch around me, heard him gasp, then felt his body push itself on.

Inside him, pumping, I reached around to grab hold of his dick. It was the rubber one, a little too stiff and too cold, but stroking that, seeing his muscular back bent away, kept things familiar. For a moment I worried that it was too strange, but he gave me no chance to falter. Gone was the quiet, the modesty. His greedy hole sucked at my dick so overwhelmingly I had to fight not to come. I thought about high school reunions, grocery lists and the DMV. I thought about tiling and grout. I thought about the boy who was starting to shiver around me, moaning, louder than was safe for our continued privacy, and dripping juice onto the hard concrete floor.

It tightened up as he came. Little spasms grabbed and released, grabbed and released at my dick. He was loud enough that I clamped my palm over his mouth, and still little grunts came. My hand grew hot from his breath. I pulled out, yanked off the plastic, and jerked until I splattered his back. He didn't wipe off, but stood to gather his clothes from the floor. Flannel went over the mess. I watched it smear under the fabric then disappear. Good. Take it home. Think of me.

He kissed me. I told him to fuck off. Had work to do. He climbed down with a smile. I had other things to worry about: the job, new cards, getting my truck. I tried to get angry again over my frustrating day, hold on to the jolt and productivity of being annoyed. It didn't work. I thought about what I'd do to that boy for breaking my concentration and grinned. If I ran into him again, I'd teach him a lesson. Show him a thing or two about what it means to wreck my bad day.

FIVE-FINGER DISCOUNT

Huck Pilgrim

Jimmy Manley wandered through the dusty aisles of Murphy Mart, a small department store at the Metro Mall. He strolled the aisles of the store's small electronics section, brushing his fingers over the boxes of video games. To a casual observer, he would appear consumed in making a selection, but this was a ruse. In fact, he was carefully scanning the store, looking for employees, trying to gauge his odds of getting away with a small theft. Jimmy liked to test himself in Murphy Mart: a small lackluster department store even in its better days, the staff here were mostly bored. He'd been caught stealing here a few times before, and the clerks had resorted to mild curses and an invitation to leave the store. One of those times, a heavy-set woman wearing a worn, harried look and a straining Murphy Mart polo shirt had caught him stuffing a hardcover book down the front of his pants. She'd smacked him in the head with the back of her hand.

"You," she'd said. "Fuck off." In her thick Russian accent, it had come out: *Joo. Fack off.*

He'd tossed the book back onto the shelf and then run from the store, only to find himself on the other side of the mall, his heart racing, unable to stop laughing. *Fack off*, indeed.

Jimmy couldn't afford to get into any more trouble: the recruiter had told him to keep his nose clean, enjoy his birthday celebration and then graduate high school. Jimmy had just turned eighteen. In a few more weeks, he'd graduate high school. And then it was good-bye Carnal, hello Recruit Training Center Great Lakes—the U.S. Naval boot camp. He'd already signed the papers.

Jimmy's father didn't want him to join the military. Jimmy had laughed at his father's initial assessment of the situation: *You'll get your head shot off*, Don Manley had said in utter dismay. Jimmy thought his father was being overly dramatic, but he didn't particularly mind. It was good to hear an opinion from the old man, even if he thought Jimmy was making a mistake. He'd enjoyed the rare treat of his father's attention.

Jimmy deftly slipped a small electronic gadget into his pants—a USB stick in the shape of a shotgun: Jimmy thought it would make a nice Father's Day gift. The cardboard backing dug into his thighs as he surveyed the store's aisles.

Meandering toward the men's clothing aisles, Jimmy found a tall mirror. Jimmy could see the outline of the package stuffed in his jeans. He skillfully adjusted himself until he was satisfied that his prize was no longer visible. He picked and fluffed at his dark curly hair. He knew all his hair would get cut off in boot camp. His head would be bald and shiny. Jimmy longed to begin his adventure in the military. He hoped to transform his slim, boyish frame into the muscled body of a real man. He squinted his big brown eyes and put on a tough grimace, but he couldn't hold it for long, breaking out into a big toothy smile. Jimmy was not much of a tough, and he knew it. Jimmy secretly hoped against hope that the military would help him transform more than just his body and his hair. He stuffed his hands in the deep pockets of his pants and wandered into the aisle of paperback books and magazines.

He picked up a fantasy novel and surreptitiously looked at the shelf of pornographic girly magazines: on one was a soft-focus picture of a beautiful girl, her breasts and thighs covered by the wide modesty wrapper of plain white paper. Jimmy could feel his cock moving in his pants. Jimmy remembered that his friend Roger Bones was also at the Metro Mall, but he didn't feel like hanging out with Roger. Each time he hung out with Roger at the Metro Mall, Jimmy ended up at some gay man's apartment, sitting on that man's couch or his bed, with his pants and underwear pooled at his ankles, a pornographic magazine in his hands, the man's mouth on him. Jimmy's cock slid to attention just thinking about it. There was good money in hustling gay men, even after Roger took his cut.

Jimmy put the novel back on the shelf. His penis pressed uncomfortably against the item in his pants, so Jimmy adjusted himself again, letting his fingers linger on his cock perhaps a little longer then he should have. He knew it was foolish, but Jimmy picked up the porno magazine and slipped its wrapper from the cover.

Jimmy hoped that his sojourn into the military would turn him into the kind of man who didn't get a raging hard-on at the thought of having his cock swallowed by a man. With chagrin, Jimmy remembered that he hadn't even been paid for the first blow job a man had given him. Unbeknownst to Jimmy, Roger had kept the money. Jimmy had incorrectly assumed the blow job itself was the reward, his payment for overcoming his fear. And in a way, that blow job was compensation of sorts: Jimmy discovered he loved to shoot his cream into the warmth of another man's mouth. So much better than firing off into his warm bedsheets, or the cold water of the toilet bowl. Once Jimmy learned there was money exchanging hands, he insisted on collecting the lion's share of the proceeds from Roger. Jimmy felt he had to. Otherwise, he would be in it just for the blow job. And that was only a very small step away from actually being gay.

Jimmy flipped through the pages of the magazine, skipping immediately to the model in the center. He luxuriated in the hard-on in his pants. He'd have to go to the mall restroom and relieve himself into one of the toilets. Jimmy tugged at the gift for his father hidden in his pants. If Jimmy's father thought he'd fail in the military, Jimmy wondered what the old man would think of his adventures with Roger in the Metro Mall? The thought made Jimmy wince, even as his cock throbbed.

Looking up from his magazine, Jimmy spotted a man striding toward him with great purpose. He was a big guy, with a wide face and flat nose. He had strong arms, a big head and chest, and steel-gray hair clipped close to his head. Jimmy felt the hard-on in his pants wither. He put the magazine back, fumbling with the paper modesty wrapper a bit before deciding to just ignore the wrapper and head for the door.

The man was fast. He must have broken into a trot as soon as Jimmy turned, because no sooner did Jimmy take a single step, then he felt a big powerful hand clamp down on his shoulder. The big man swiftly positioned himself between Jimmy and the arch leading into the mall, and then he looked evenly at Jimmy, sizing him up. Jimmy grinned sheepishly. He had a square jaw and deep-blue eyes. He wore dark slacks and a button-down blue oxford shirt, cuffs rolled halfway up his thick, hairy, tattoo-covered forearms.

"You come with me," he said. Again, a thick accent, Russian

or Eastern European. "You vit me," the man said. Stepping toward Jimmy, the man used his superior size to intimidate the boy. Jimmy noticed the name badge pinned to the man's deep chest: BOGDON.

"I wasn't doing anything, mister," Jimmy said. "Honest." The man looked at the pornographic magazine hastily stashed in the rack, but he didn't say anything. Jimmy's face flushed furiously. "I was just looking," he stammered.

"S'okay," the man said, his face softening. "It's okay." He was nodding his head and had relaxed his voice, but he put his big hand on Jimmy's thin biceps. "Come," the guard said. "Come. We talk." He started to hustle Jimmy farther into the store. Jimmy went with the man, this Bogdon, feeling light-headed, butterflies raging in his belly. What would his father say? The recruiter? What about his plans to change himself? Bogdon walked Jimmy through a door marked EMPLOYEES ONLY, to a small room with an even smaller table, some chairs and a lot of video monitoring equipment.

"Put on table," Bogdon said, after he had closed the door. He stood with both his hands clasped in front of him.

"I wasn't doing anything, mister," Jimmy said.

Bogdon smiled. He lowered his head. He waited.

"*Really*," Jimmy whined. His mouth was dry. He hated how weak and pathetic his voice sounded, even to him. He sighed. Hung his head. Sighed again.

Reaching into his pants, Jimmy pulled out the gift he had stolen for his father. Tossed it onto the table.

"More?" Bogdon said softly.

"No more," Jimmy whispered. He heard his own voice crack a little and he hoped he wouldn't cry.

"This what happens now," Bogdon said. "You lean over table. You keep both hands behind back. I must look." Jimmy looked at the table. "You understand?" Bogdon said.

Jimmy nodded. "You're going to search me," he said.

Bogdon smiled. He was an older guy, probably about fifty. Jimmy wondered how many times Bogdon had had to search the people who shoplifted from Murphy Mart. Jimmy leaned over the table, pressing his cheek against the smooth wood finish. He put his hands behind his back, letting the table take all of his weight. It was an awkward, humiliating position to assume, and he closed his eyes.

Jimmy felt Bogdon's big hand on his wrists.

"I must do this," Bogdon said.

Jimmy felt the cold metal of handcuffs and immediately tried to stand. Bogdon put his other hand on Jimmy's back, forcing the wind out of him.

"Don't," Jimmy said. "Please."

Bogdon pressed his hip into Jimmy's backside and held his wrists fast. He kept his hand in the middle of Jimmy's back until Jimmy let his body go limp. "I must," Bogdon said. Taking his hand off Jimmy's back, Bogdon kept his hip pressed up against the boy. Jimmy heard the first metallic lock click into place and then the next. With Jimmy's hands secured, Bogdon turned his own body, so that his groin was pressed against the boy's bottom.

"Hold on," Bogdon said. "I fix handcuffs so your wrists don't get no hurt." Jimmy could feel Bogdon fiddling with the handcuffs. Bogdon had himself pressed tightly up against Jimmy. It wasn't physically uncomfortable, but Jimmy was aware that Bogdon was unabashedly pressing his groin into Jimmy's hip. Was he afraid Jimmy would race from the little room with his hands shackled behind his back? Jimmy snorted softly at the thought.

"You okay?" Bogdon asked. "Wrist good?"

"Good," Jimmy croaked. "Good." He wanted to get it over with.

"Okay," Bogdon muttered. "Now I check you out."

With that, Bogdon placed both his hands on Jimmy's right arm: one hand on Jimmy's shoulder, the other under his armpit. Bogdon slowly and methodically moved his hands down Jimmy's arm to his elbow, then finally to his wrist. Bogdon sighed. He moved to Jimmy's left arm, and did the same thing, keeping his groin pressed into Jimmy's bottom. Jimmy had never been searched before, but he was sure this search was inappropriate. He was only wearing a T-shirt, for heaven's sake. He wanted to say something, but he wasn't quite sure how to put it into words, so instead he just sighed loudly.

Bogdon shushed him. "Easy, my little dove," he whispered. "Easy." Muttering softly to himself, Bogdon put his hands on Jimmy's torso, slowly working them down to the boy's hips. At one point, Bogdon repositioned himself so that his groin was over the boy's manacled hands, and then Bogdon leaned forward and reached under Jimmy's chest. Jimmy was aware where his hands were in relation to Bogdon's penis, and even though Jimmy couldn't feel anything, he was uncomfortable. Both his nipples were "accidently" tweaked, between Bogdon's thumb and hand, as he ran his palms adroitly over Jimmy's slim torso.

Jimmy gasped. He could feel his cock start to respond. Most of his apprehension at being detained suddenly evaporated. He wondered if Bogdon were gay. If Bogdon were gay, Jimmy thought he might be able to turn the tables. Maybe even take advantage of the situation. Come out a little ahead.

Bogdon put one of his hand on the inside of Jimmy's left thigh, the other on the outside Jimmy's leg. Bogdon pressed the inside hand up against Jimmy's crotch, jostling the boy's balls.

Jimmy inhaled deeply. He would gladly let Bogdon suck his dick in exchange for his freedom. Jimmy felt that the best way to communicate this to Bogdon might be without words, by using his body instead. Fortunately, Jimmy could feel his cock already beginning to throb. He tried to coax an even better erection from himself: his thoughts moved to the model he'd been looking at in the magazine, to some of the girls he knew in high school, and even to the lusty drawings of warrior women in a graphic novel he enjoyed. Bogdon's hands had reached Jimmy's ankle, but Jimmy had still only managed a small rise in his pants. His anxiety began to mount. Bogdon switched to Jimmy's other ankle and slowly began working his way up the leg. This was a clutch moment that called for desperate measures. Jimmy let his mind wander to the last time he let a man suck his cock. The guy had gotten Jimmy good and hard, and then he'd stopped, sucked his finger to get it wet, and slipped it into Jimmy's sweaty ass. Jimmy hadn't expected that. Pressing his heels into the bed, he'd raised his ass high from the bed, and almost immediately ejaculated into the man's mouth. It had been one of the most erotic experiences of his young life. Jimmy didn't like to think about it, but now that he had, his cock was a heavy log in his pants. Bogdon let his hand rub against Jimmy's nuts.

When he felt the man's touch, Jimmy exhaled loudly.

The old man chuckled. And then Jimmy felt Bogdon's hand cup his entire cock. Bogdon made a lusty sigh and gently squeezed Jimmy's manhood. Jimmy mewled.

"You like," Bogdon said.

Bogdon placed his big hands on Jimmy's shoulders and effortlessly raised him to his feet. He helped Jimmy into a nearby chair, his hands still locked behind his back. Jimmy wasn't really sure what to say or do next, so he decided to play the coquette: he pushed his rump to the edge of the seat and leaned back in his chair, his hands gripping the back edge of the seat. He let his eyelids half cover his eyes. He didn't want to overplay it, but he rocked his hips slightly and enjoyed the sensation of his hard cock rubbing against his underwear.

"You want me let you go?" Bogdon whispered. A half smile played on his lips. Jimmy's heart soared in his chest. He swallowed hard, pursing his lips. Smiling slyly, Jimmy nodded. "Please," he asked sweetly. Bogdon was grinning and had his hands on his hips.

"You do me the pleasure?" Bogdon asked. "You do me the pleasure, I let you go free."

Jimmy grinned. He'd never heard anyone call it that before, but he opened his knees wide. He invited the old man in. Jimmy found that when he gave himself over to the idea of receiving head from a man, his anxiety about his own sexuality disappeared. His lust seemed capable of transporting him to a special place where all that mattered was the relief of the hard cock in his pants. He bit his lip and rocked his hips. He may have even moaned.

Bogdon grinned. And then he quickly unbuckled his belt, opened his pants and lowered his fly.

Jimmy sat bolt upright in the chair. His eyes were open wide now, the coquettish smile gone from his lips.

Bogdon pulled his cock from his pants and stroked it. He had an uncut penis and it was only half hard. As he stroked it, the head disappeared into his shaft, only to reappear a few seconds later, glistening and round. His cock wasn't massive, but it was well proportioned and thick, and he had a nice, dark coloring. Bogdon proudly stroked it.

"Wait, wait," Jimmy said breathlessly. "There's been a mistake." He was grappling with what he had expected to happen, and what was actually happening instead. "You don't understand," Jimmy said. He laughed nervously. "I'm not gay," Jimmy said, his voice sounding high and squeaky in his ears. Bogdon laughed.

"Mister, mister," Jimmy said anxiously. He was being misunderstood and he could feel the situation spinning out of control. He was feeling frantic, beside himself. Bogdon chuckled and took a step closer to the chair, his cock pointing at Jimmy's face like a weapon.

"*Bogdon*," Jimmy said sharply. Bogdon stopped stroking himself. "I can't," Jimmy said. "I'm not gay. I'm mean, I'm no queer."

Bogdon tilted his head. He looked at Jimmy as if this were the first time he had seen him. Bogdon put his meaty hand on Jimmy's shoulder. Leaning down, Bogdon reached between Jimmy's legs and found his cock. The boy had lost some of his erection, but he was still somewhat aroused. Bogdon grinned. He rubbed the boy's penis, which thickened at his touch.

"You can, my dove," he said. "You can. Is no big deal. Is like sucking thumb. Only, instead of thumb," Bogdon chuckled, "you suck *cock*." Jimmy groaned and turned his head.

"No," Jimmy whispered. A silence followed. Bogdon stood, gently squeezing Jimmy's shoulder. Jimmy kept his head turned to the wall. Bogdon toyed with a curl in the boy's hair.

"I'm not gay," Jimmy squeaked.

"You don't have to be gay," Bogdon whispered sympathetically. Jimmy felt his cock lurch involuntarily. He squeezed his thighs together. Bogdon watched the boy squirm in his seat.

"No one will know," Bogdon said softly. Jimmy inhaled deeply. Looked at his feet. Stealing a glance at Bogdon, he pushed the air from his lungs slowly. Bogdon toyed idly with his cock. He kept his eyes on the boy.

Jimmy looked up at Bogdon. Looked him right in his blue eyes. "Please," Jimmy begged, his tone desperate. "Please." Bogdon smiled. His cock seemed to thicken at the boy's plea.

"Is nothing can be done," Bogdon said firmly. "You must decide."

Jimmy sighed. Ran his tongue around his lips. Opened his mouth just a bit. He closed his mouth to swallow, and then he opened it again. He turned his head to face Bogdon's cock. Opening his mouth wider, Jimmy tilted his head and closed his eyes. He could feel his own erection throbbing in his pants. Jimmy paused briefly, his mouth an inch from Bogdon's cock. He could feel the warmth from the man's cock on his lips.

And then Jimmy simply moved his head forward, and for the first time in his entire life, he had a cock in his mouth. He gave himself a moment to get used to it. Bogdon's cock was warm, and it filled Jimmy's mouth completely: It was on his tongue and up against the roof of his mouth and nuzzled against his molars. Jimmy found he had to breathe through his nose. He smelled the musky, not unpleasant odor of a man. Jimmy tasted nothing at first, but then his mouth began to salivate, and he noticed Bogdon had a mild salty taste.

Bogdon sighed appreciatively.

Jimmy opened his eyes and saw the tiny, tight gray curls of Bogdon's pubic patch. Bogdon was busily opening the buttons of his shirt, tugging his white cotton undershirt high, exposing his hairy belly. For an old man, he was in great shape. He ran his hands over his flat stomach and his cock seemed to grow even thicker in Jimmy's mouth.

Jimmy understood what was expected, but he wasn't sure exactly what to do. He hesitantly rocked his head, his mind still reeling with the fact that he had somehow been convinced to take a cock in his mouth. He thought of what his father might say and grew anxious. He panicked. Leaning back in his chair, Jimmy let Bogdon's penis fall from his mouth.

"Can I stop?" Jimmy whispered, his breath coming heavy. "Is that good? Can I go home now?" Bogdon chuckled softly. He shook his wet cock. Sighed. He pointed to one of the monitors mounted on the wall where a host of similar small black-and-white monitors were mounted. "You see here?" Bogdon said. Jimmy saw a uniformed security guard walking down a long corridor.

"Now watch here," Bogdon said, pointing to another monitor that showed a different corridor somewhere. "Wait, wait. Watch," Bogdon said, as he saw Jimmy's interest wane. As they waited, Bogdon rummaged through the bottom drawer of an old wooden desk and dug out a magazine, which he kept folded in half in his hand.

"You see," Bogdon said, his attention back on the monitor. The same uniformed guard from the earlier monitor appeared and ambled down the hall. "That is my partner," Bogdon smiled. He let his T-shirt fall down over his stomach. His pants were still open, and the T-shirt covered much of his crotch as well. "He will be here, in this room, in, ah, maybe..." Bogdon looked at the monitors and considered. "Twenty minutes?" He shrugged his shoulders, as if to say, give or take a few minutes.

"We must be finished before he arrives," Bogdon said. As he said this, he moved closer to Jimmy in the chair. "And to finish," Bogdon smiled down at Jimmy. "You must make me come."

Jimmy swallowed hard. "And if I don't make it?" Jimmy asked. He felt pretty sure he already knew the answer.

"Deal off," Bogdon said. "Partner here, I must call police." Bogdon opened his magazine and began to leaf through its pages. He sighed, reached between his legs and lazily stroked himself. Jimmy could see the cover of the magazine in Bogdon's hands featured a buxom blonde on her knees with a ball gag in her mouth.

Jimmy thought about his options. He could let himself get arrested and then tell the police Bogdon had asked him to suck cock. Was that even a crime? Jimmy doubted it. And even if it were, his father and the recruiter were both sure to find out. Not to mention all of his friends at school. Jimmy sighed. He'd already had Bogdon's cock in his mouth. Even if he got busted for stealing, nothing could change the fact that he'd already sucked a cock. *He was a cocksucker.* Jimmy became aware of his own erection in his pants. He squeezed his legs together and enjoyed the feeling of his thighs pressing against his shaft. He would just have to finish. It was his only recourse. As soon as he thought it, he knew it was the right decision.

Leaning forward, Jimmy took Bogdon back into his mouth. Bogdon sighed. He reached down and raised his T-shirt to give Jimmy better access to his cock, but otherwise he kept his head in his magazine. Jimmy knew everything depended upon his own ability to quickly pick up cocksucking skills. It was all up to him. He had to suck this old man off. He started to work his head methodically back and forth. He quickly realized his biggest problem: he needed his hands.

"Bogdon," Jimmy said, looking up. "Free my hands." Bogdon tilted his magazine back to see the boy's face. He grinned. He turned the magazine over to show Jimmy the picture he was looking at: a woman on her knees with her hands bound behind her back, her mouth on the cock of a man standing in front of her.

Bogdon chuckled. "No," he said. "I don't think so," and resumed his reading. Jimmy licked his lips. Bogdon was being cruel, but Jimmy couldn't worry about that now. He went into problem solving mode. Any apprehension he had felt about sucking cock was gone, replaced by the logistical challenges and limitations before him. While Jimmy was an inexperienced cocksucker, Bogdon was already pretty hard. And he'd been stiff for a while. Jimmy felt that his best shot was to make his mouth as wet as possible, and then use his slippery mouth to get in as many strokes as he could.

Jimmy scooped Bogdon's cock back into his mouth. He nuzzled it, letting his mouth fill with saliva. He started to rock his head. Soon he could hear wet noises and felt his own spit dribbling down his chin. Occasionally Jimmy would stop sucking, open his mouth, and slurp the spit that was leaking out of his mouth. He did this to keep his mouth well-lubricated: he was a boy-powered, cocksucking machine. The muscles in his neck began to ache. Jimmy mewled and moaned with Bogdon's cock in his mouth. At first, Jimmy made these noises because his own cock was hard, and it was rubbing against his underwear, and it made him feel so wonderful that he just had to moan. But then Jimmy eventually realized that Bogdon was enjoying his moans, too. Whether it was the sound of Jimmy's moaning that turned on Bogdon, or the vibrations from Jimmy's mouth on Bogdon's hard cock, Jimmy couldn't be sure. All he knew was that he needed to continue moaning, as much for Bogdon's pleasure as for his own. Jimmy put all he had into sucking the fat cock in his mouth.

Bogdon sighed. He tossed away his magazine and raised his shirt. He grabbed his cock in his hand, and put the other hand on the top of Jimmy's head. Bogdon positioned himself so that only the head of his cock was in Jimmy's mouth. Jimmy felt relieved and stopped bobbing his head. Jimmy could feel the saliva running freely down his chin.

"Okay," Bogdon said. "Okay" Jimmy rested. His jaw hurt, his neck was sore. He wondered how much longer he could have sustained the pace that he had set for himself. He felt so grateful to let it all go. To simply sit in the chair and let Bogdon take over. "Okay," Bogdon said again, in the clipped cadence of a man working himself towards orgasm, fucking Jimmy's mouth with short, quick thrusts. Jimmy knew what was coming: Bogdon would soon fill his mouth with warm cum. He had known that was coming all along, but had forced the thought to the back of his mind. Everything had happened so fast. There was no time to negotiate. And now his choice seemed gone: if Jimmy pulled his head back now, Bogdon might not finish before his partner arrived. And besides the timing, there was also no guarantee that Bogdon would throw his effort into the mix were Jimmy to stop once more. Jimmy didn't think he had it in him to bring Bogdon to the brink again, solo. No, it was far too risky for Jimmy to ask for a halt. Jimmy thought it might be best to just let things run their course. To take whatever the old man had to give. To receive his load.

While Jimmy secretly relished the idea of being forced to swallow, he also felt a little terrified. He allowed himself to whimper. Jimmy looked up at Bogdon with big brown moist eyes, and Bogdon had to have known what was in the boy's heart. Perhaps it was even this very knowledge that sent Bogdon over the edge.

"Swallow," Bogdon said softly, his voice thick with lust. Jimmy felt the warm cum at the back of his throat. And swallow he did. He gulped, in fact, to prevent himself from choking. And he twisted in his seat, all the better to feel the erection in his pants, rubbing against his thighs. "Swallow it all, little dove," Bogdon said. "Swallow it all for me." Jimmy flexed his buttocks, pressing his cock into his jeans. He swallowed numerous times, as many as it took, until Bogdon finally stopped shooting into Jimmy's mouth. When Bogdon's orgasm finished, he sighed heavily, then softly chuckled. He reassembled his clothes and looked to the monitors to assess his remaining time.

And Jimmy sat quietly, still swallowing; only this time it was his own saliva he accepted, a bid to temper the salty aftertaste in his mouth. When Bogdon had finished with his clothing, he leaned against the table. He put both his hands in his lap. He sighed.

"Stand," he said, addressing the boy. Jimmy did as he was told, his head hanging. "Will you unlock me?" he asked. He did not look up.

"Soon," Bogdon said. "Come first." Bogdon waved him forward with small finger motions. Jimmy wasn't sure what Bogdon wanted. The space was small. The place where he was standing was only a pace or two away from Bogdon. "Come," Bogdon said. Jimmy took a step forward.

Bogdon reached out and grabbed the belt buckle of Jimmy's pants. He gently tugged the boy forward, until Jimmy had to straddle Bogdon's thigh. Jimmy looked up, his eyes wet.

"I'm not gay," Jimmy hissed. Bogdon did not laugh. He simply took Jimmy's hips in his hands and pulled the boy against his own sturdy thigh. Jimmy could feel his hard cock pressed against the man's warm leg. Jimmy squirmed in protest, but it did little good to win his release: his hands were still locked behind his back and Bogdon held him in his powerful arms.

"Come," Bogdon whispered. "Come for me." Jimmy finally realized Bogdon wanted him to come. To shoot his cum into his pants. That was okay with Jimmy. He wanted to come. Badly. He wanted to stain his underwear and his pants. His protestations turned into awkward attempts to rub himself against Bogdon. But Jimmy found his position awkward. The only way that he could get his hips to move in the way he needed was to let himself go. To let the man before him take his full body weight. Jimmy knew there was very little time left. After a few unsuccessful bids to start a rhythm on his feet, he finally did it. He let himself go. He fell into Bogdon's big tattooed arms.

And the big man held Jimmy as he squirmed, and his orgasm came quickly. Bogdon laughed as he felt the boy's body stiffen. Jimmy nuzzled his face into Bogdon's neck. Jimmy made a satisfied groan and came in his pants, feeling the warm semen spread against his own groin and leg. Bogdon held Jimmy for what felt to Jimmy like an eternity, a blissful infinity. Jimmy could smell the old man's cologne. He let it fill his head.

Finally Bogdon pulled the boy to his feet. He stood behind Jimmy, turning him toward the door. Bogdon reached into his pants pocket and then whispered into Jimmy's ear: "Listen to me: Do not. Hit me." Jimmy hadn't expected that warning. He craned his neck.

Bogdon unlocked his wrists. When his hands were free, Jimmy rubbed them.

"Go," Bogdon said. "Hurry. Partner coming." Jimmy opened the door. He stood on the threshold for a moment. His pants were wet. The cum was cooling and he felt vaguely embarrassed to wear a huge stain of cum out into the mall. He looked back into the little room, where Bogdon still stood; and something swelled in Jimmy's chest. He opened his mouth to say something and then thought better of it. Instead, he raced the few steps between him and Bogdon. The big man flinched in surprise. He leaned back with his eyebrows high. Throwing his arms around Bogdon's neck, Jimmy let his body follow, pressing himself up against the big man's sturdy frame. Jimmy held Bogdon for a moment, then Jimmy stepped back and let his hands come down over Bogdon's stubbly cheeks.

With his hands framing Bogdon's face, Jimmy stood on tiptoe and kissed Bogdon full on the mouth. Jimmy pressed his tongue against Bogdon's lips, but the old man wouldn't kiss Jimmy back that way, whether it was because the kiss was too much of a surprise, or because Bogdon didn't kiss men with an open mouth, Jimmy couldn't say for sure.

Jimmy laughed. Didn't matter. He raced from the little room and then down the dimly lit hall that was for employees only and finally out into Murphy Mart. He passed the security guard he'd seen in the monitor, and Jimmy waved his fingers and just kept right on running. He ran until he reached the other side of the mall and then he stopped running and started laughing. Jimmy briefly considered stealing a pair of jeans to replace his cum-stained pants. But he knew he had to stay out of trouble. He knew he had to keep his nose clean. But now he also knew that sometimes a little bit of risk could be a good thing.

Sometimes a little jeopardy was exactly what a boy needed most.

MY BEST FRIEND'S DAD

J. M. Snyder

The first man I ever fell in love with was my best friend's dad. Mikey didn't know about it, of course, and neither did Mr. Pierce.

The dad was nothing like the son. I'd known Mikey since kindergarten, when he pushed me off the swing set on the school playground and had to sit in time-out for the rest of recess. His dad had a hard voice: rough, burned out from too many late evenings with his friends huddled around the dining room table, cigarette smoke stinging their throats and watering their eyes as they played hand after hand of poker. Whenever I stayed over on one of those nights, Mikey and I were confined to his room upstairs, out of the way, though not out of earshot. The men's raucous laughter and coarse language made us envious. How I longed to have Mr. Pierce call me a dirty bastard one second, then clap me on the back and roar with approval at something I'd said the next.

Though most boys outgrew sleepovers once they reached

high school, I still stayed at Mikey's house a few nights every month. It got me out of my own home, and it gave me a chance to be close to Mr. Pierce, who probably never said two words to us on the nights I was there, but any small glimpse, any gesture, fueled my teenage crush. I wasn't too worried about the kids at school finding out I slept over at Mikey's, because we'd been friends for so long most people assumed we were a set. Wherever Mikey went, I wasn't far behind.

The last time I spent the night was the Saturday before I left for college. My mother had begun to get weepy whenever she saw me, sniffling into a tissue and babbling about losing her "baby boy." Please, I was eighteen, and the college I'd be attending was only a two-hour drive away, but to hear her tell it, I was practically taking classes on the moon. When Mikey called to see if I wanted to come on over, just for pizza and a movie, I couldn't pack an overnight bag fast enough.

Sleeping over at Mikey's meant an evening leafing through porno mags, playing video games and watching horror movies on DVD. Mr. Pierce's poker buddies started showing up around six. While Mikey and I duked it out on one of his wrestling games for the PlayStation and kicked the shit out of each other, I could hear the men downstairs laughing and cussing. As much as I liked Mikey's company, I wished I could join them.

We lost track of time. Finally Mikey tossed the controller aside and gave me a wicked grin. "How about you sneak downstairs and grab some beers out of the fridge?"

I gave him an incredulous look. "What? Hell, no. What if someone sees me?"

Mikey stood, stretched, and flopped sideways onto his bed, the springs creaking beneath his weight. Flicking up the bottom of his curtain, he craned his neck to look out at the street below. "Two of the cars are gone," he said as he rolled onto his back.

"It's kind of late. I think the card game's over. No one will see you."

"Your dad," I argued. I hadn't heard Mr. Pierce's heavy footsteps on the stairs, which meant he hadn't gone to bed.

But Mikey shrugged that off, too. "Probably passed out on the couch in the den. You'll be fine. Just go down, grab two bottles and run back up here. If he sees you, tell him you're getting something to drink. He doesn't have to know what."

I still didn't want to do it, but I couldn't see any flaws in Mikey's logic or any reason why I *couldn't* do it without looking bad.

"Come on," Mikey cajoled. "What's he going to say? You probably won't even see him."

Pushing myself up on my feet, I announced, "I have to take a leak." I'd worry about the beers when I came back from the bathroom.

The moment I stepped into the hall, Mikey's braying laugh erupted behind me as he shoved the bedroom door shut. I heard the insidious *click* as he locked me out. Angry, I stormed across the hall into the bathroom and kicked the door shut behind me. "Asshole."

Looked like I was going downstairs after all.

I considered hammering on Mikey's door until he had no other choice but to open up. Then I figured Mr. Pierce would hear the commotion and come upstairs to yell at us, so I settled for hitting Mikey's closed door with my fist, which set him snickering inside the bedroom—I know, I heard him when I pressed my ear to the wood. "You're dead," I growled, my mouth against the doorjamb. "See if I bring you any beer."

"You better!" Mikey hollered. The closeness of his voice startled me—he was right on the other side of the door. I wriggled the knob but it didn't turn, which meant he held it tight to keep it from rattling. "You ain't getting back in here without at least two beers. One for each of us."

I waited, silent, until I could hear him breathing; he must've pressed an ear to the door, listening to see if I'd left or not. So I hit the door again, harder this time, and heard a satisfying "Ow!"

Before he could open the door to retaliate, I hurried downstairs.

The first few steps disappeared quickly beneath my feet, but halfway down I paused. The darkness wasn't as complete as I had first thought. The lights in the living room were out, and if I moved a little to the left, I saw the kitchen was dark as well. But another step brought me closer to the bottom of the stairs, where I saw a warm glow of light spread in a small circle from the doorway where the living room and dining room met. As I crept closer, one step at a time, I realized that the folding louvered doors separating one room from the next had been pulled shut.

That gave me pause. The glow I saw came from under the door, where the wood was warped just enough that it didn't sit flush against the floor.

Straining to hear anything, I held my breath and listened. Someone cleared his throat, a discreet sound that told me Mr. Pierce was still in the dining room. Cards purred as he shuffled them, and a few poker chips clattered to the table as if he'd been stacking them out of boredom and they'd finally fallen over. But there was no other sound—no one talking to him, no nervous scuffling, nothing to indicate he wasn't alone in there. If he caught me...

At the bottom of the stairs, I peeked around the wall to get a good look in the kitchen. To my surprise, those louvered doors were also shut, though they didn't close all the way and the gap they left between the wall and the door allowed a shaft of light to penetrate the darkened kitchen. It illuminated an empty beer bottle that had been left on the counter so it cast an amber glow over the sink's faucet. If I were quick, I could probably sneak in there, open the fridge really slowly so it wouldn't make any noise, grab two bottles of beer and dash back upstairs before Mr. Pierce even knew I was there.

My socked feet were silent as I inched across the carpet onto the tiled floor of the kitchen. My heart hammered in my chest, every nerve was on end, and my hair felt puffed in fear all along my arms and the back of my neck. If I were caught...

I wouldn't be caught. In my mind's eye I could see myself getting the beers. I crept closer, watched my hand reaching for the refrigerator door, felt cool metal as my fingers closed around the handle. I wouldn't get caught. I *wouldn't...*

From the dining room came that sound again, half cough, half clearing the throat. With a voice steeped in gravel, Mr. Pierce spoke. "So you owe me what, three hundred?"

My hand froze on the handle. *Oh, fuck.* He wasn't alone.

I heard another sound, something sexy, a mingled laugh and moan. "Three-fifty. Don't round it down just because you're hard for me."

The words drew me closer. Without conscious thought, I relaxed my grip on the handle of the fridge and turned toward the partially shut louvered door. "*Hard* for me?" Was that what he had said?

Oh, Jesus.

I expected an angry shout, a denial, something fast and quick that sent this fellow packing. Instead, I was surprised to hear the hint of a smile in Mr. Pierce's voice when he answered, "I was cutting you some slack. I know you ain't got the cash."

With a throaty chuckle, his friend replied, "I know it's not cash you want from me."

I couldn't help it—my feet moved forward, heading for the louvered door. I stopped at the counter and tried to peer around the gap where the door and jamb didn't quite meet, but all I saw was blank wall. Were they talking about what I *thought* they were talking about? What I *hoped* they were talking about?

Then I heard muffled moans, a slight gasp, indistinct words. I inched closer and prized the louvers up slowly, careful not to let them squeak. Through the wooden slats I saw Mr. Pierce sitting at the head of the dining room table. He was turned toward me, facing a friend of his I recognized as RC, who sat on the bench closest to the kitchen, the same seat Mikey always preferred to use. Only RC wasn't exactly sitting any longer. Both hands leaned heavily on Mr. Pierce's thighs, rumpling the work pants he wore as RC fisted the dark blue material. RC stretched above Mr. Pierce, face buried in his neck, and as I watched, Mr. Pierce's thick lips parted in a low, guttural moan. One hand rubbed over RC's strong arm, kneading through his shirt. The other trailed down RC's chest to tug at the waistband of RC's jeans.

Suddenly my own jeans felt two sizes too small. Without thinking about it, I thumbed open the fly and felt the zipper part beneath the erection straining at my crotch. My whole body flushed at the sensation of my hard dick released from confinement and I pressed my palm against it before my fingers encircled my shaft through the cotton of my briefs.

When RC's mouth covered Mr. Pierce's, I bit my lower lip to keep from whimpering. *Yes,* I prayed. *Thank you, God, for letting me see this.*

Apparently Mr. Pierce didn't share my appreciation. With his hand flat against RC's chest, he held the younger man at bay. "Sweet as they are," he purred, "your kisses aren't enough to pay your debt."

"You're the one who knocked off fifty bucks." The coy smile I heard in RC's voice excited me and I rubbed the front of my briefs, which had grown damp beneath my growing erection.

Mr. Pierce's laugh was like a warm hand that wrapped around my balls and squeezed gently. I almost moaned at the sound, but bit down harder on my lip to keep quiet. "I can get these for free whenever I want," he murmured.

The thought of these two men doing this—*this!*—after every card party with Mikey and me upstairs, ignorant, made me want to weep. I had never loved anyone as much as I did the both of them, right at that instant. Though I knew I should just tiptoe back up to Mikey's room without a word, before they knew I was there, nothing could force me to move. I wanted to see this, I *had* to see it.

My hand slipped into the waistband of my briefs. My fingers smoothed down the kinked curls at my crotch, then strummed along the stiffening length jutting from my unzipped fly. When my thumb rubbed over the tip of my cock, I whimpered a little with desire. Oh, hell yes. I needed this.

In the dining room, RC had folded one leg beneath him and now sat perched on the bench before Mr. Pierce, whose spread legs and slouched posture looked like an invitation I knew I would have never been able to resist. With sure hands RC explored the wide expanse of Mr. Pierce's chest, flattening his undershirt flush against his flesh. At the waistband of his pants, RC untucked the shirt, plucking it free from the belt buckle, and flicked it up to expose a pale swath of stomach. My fist tightened around my cock at seeing the hair swirled around his navel, black and gray as if seasoned just right; the slight paunch from the way he sat, the hint of belly fat that pooched over the top of his belt, the way the skin seemed to quiver when RC's fingers tickled over it. Leaning down, RC pressed his face to

Mr. Pierce's stomach and rested his cheek in the tufts of hair as he snuggled close.

Jealousy flooded me. *I* wanted to be there, held in the safety of Mr. Pierce's embrace, clutched tight to the man I had loved all these years. My cock ached at the thought of doing that, *just* that, and nothing else. I stroked myself as I watched RC's lips pucker and kiss Mr. Pierce wherever he could reach without moving—belly, navel, the underside of one pectoral muscle that peeked out from beneath the shirt.

Pressing his mouth against Mr. Pierce's skin, RC suddenly blew a wet raspberry, the sound loud and startling in the silence.

Mr. Pierce growled as he shoved RC back and wiped at the slobber on his stomach. "Come on," he muttered, sounding exactly like Mikey when my friend wanted me to do something and I was too busy being silly to comply. "Are we going to do this, or what? Because you can leave."

RC's hands found Mr. Pierce's belt buckle. The teasing grin on his face made my whole body flush. "You don't want me to go."

Mr. Pierce grunted in reply, but stayed silent. With expert ease RC unbuckled the belt and let it fall open, then unzipped the front of Mr. Pierce's work pants. I leaned forward, squinting through the louvers, holding my breath as one word tripped like a litany through my mind. *Please, please, pleasepleaseplease.*

He tugged open Mr. Pierce's fly, pushing the material down out of the way as he parted it. Dingy white briefs appeared in the gap, rising like dough over Mr. Pierce's erection. I had to grip the counter with my free hand as I fondled my dick, my underwear chafing now, my body trilling with desire. Gently RC rolled down the top of Mr. Pierce's briefs, and the large cock that swung into view was ruddy and veined and so goddamn *huge* that I squeezed my balls when I saw it. When RC leaned down to rub that thick length against his cheek, I wanted to rush in there, push him aside and take his place.

I wanted that to be *me*.

I watched, giddy and light-headed, as he wrapped his tongue around the base of Mr. Pierce's shaft. I wondered what such flesh tasted like—I pictured myself in that position, head in Mr. Pierce's lap, tongue buried in the graying hair of his crotch. It was *my* tongue I saw slide up the length of his cock, my tongue that swirled around the bulbous tip, my tongue that dipped down the dribbling slit before my mouth opened wide to take him in.

As RC went down on Mr. Pierce, I gasped. I pushed my underwear below my balls and squatted a bit, leaning back against the counter to get comfortable. My erect dick hardened in the cool air, my nuts hanging low between my legs, and I licked my palms, first one, then the other, before resuming massaging my own length. The spittle helped, easing the friction. My fingers flew over familiar territory as not five feet away, Mr. Pierce leaned back in his seat, a blissful smile on his face while RC sucked his cock. This was my daydream come true, my fantasies made real. It was me in there with him, my throat working his erection, my fist tight around the base of his shaft, my fingers rubbing under his scrotum to rim the hairy darkness at his core.

In all my eighteen years, I had never seen a man pleasured by another. Oh, I had seen pictures—those magazines under my bed had their fair share of cum-flecked and dog-eared pages, to be sure. But they were staged images, hard cocks that had been stroked and polished until they gleamed for the cameras. All the pinups were solo shots, not couples. I didn't Google gay porn online because the last way I wanted to come out to my family was by someone—my mother perhaps, or a teacher at school—discovering the websites I had visited recently. I knew gay porn existed; I just didn't have access to it. RC's kiss was the first time I ever saw two men show any affection toward each other that extended beyond a handshake or a clap on the back. So this, *this*—Mr. Pierce shoved deep into RC's willing mouth, one hand holding the back of RC's neck, the other cradling RC's unshaven cheek...this was my first glimpse of heaven.

After several long minutes, Mr. Pierce clenched his hand into a fist at RC's nape. The next time RC bobbed up, the hand on his face eased beneath his jaw, holding him back. The look Mr. Pierce gave RC smoldered—even across the distance that separated us, I felt that look deep in my groin and had to bite into the fleshy base of my thumb to keep from crying out with want. "Damn, you're good," Mr. Pierce said, his voice soft.

My cheeks blazed at the compliment as if it had been directed toward me.

A slow smile softened Mr. Pierce's stern features. "But you know what I want."

RC laughed and turned his face to press his mouth in Mr. Pierce's palm, planting a kiss there. "What you *always* want. A piece of my ass."

There was the slightest hint of a tease in Mr. Pierce's voice when he countered, "It's an oh-so-fuckable ass."

"You like it?" RC asked.

My mind whirled out in a blind rush. *Oh, god. Oh, my god. They aren't...they won't...please please please yes.*

In a seductive purr, Mr. Pierce admitted, "I love it."

My hand tightened around my aching dick. *Yes, yes, yes.*

In one fluid motion RC stood, hands opening his fly as he turned and shucked down his jeans. He bent over slightly, mooning Mr. Pierce and giving me a good look at those plump, dimpled cheeks. His ass was smooth and tanned, with a hint of dark hair curving beneath each buttock to trail into the crack between them. A mole sat like a beauty mark just below the tailbone on his right buttock, one single imperfection on an otherwise flawless canvas. "If you love it so much," RC joked, "why don't you kiss it?"

My whole body throbbed with need. *Yes.*

When Mr. Pierce leaned forward, his stiff cock poked his belly, the damp tip smearing the trail of hair below his navel. His large hands caught RC's hips, pulling the younger man closer; his lips puckered, straining forward as he aimed for RC's ass. His mouth closed over that small mole with a loud *smack!* I could hear from where I sat. My fingers flew along my dick, jerking it sore, seeking release as I panted, watching, wanting more.

As if he heard my silent plea, Mr. Pierce obliged. Spreading RC's buttocks apart, he licked out to taste the dark skin hidden between them. In fascination I watched that tongue wet a path down, *down*—I could almost feel it on my own ass, which trembled for such a touch. It'd be warm, and softer than a man had a right to be, the saliva cooling along my flesh almost instantly. Mr. Pierce buried his nose between those ripe mounds, his jaw widening as his tongue angled down between them. I saw that tongue flick in and out beneath RC's left cheek and could only imagine just where it tickled when out of sight.

All coyness had left RC's face. He now leaned heavily against the dining room table, both palms flat on cards and poker chips alike. His head was thrown back, a look of sheer ecstasy written on his features. "Yes," he panted, arching his butt into Mr. Pierce's face. His feet slid apart as he tried to spread his legs wider. "God, yes. Right there, Hank. That's it. That's the spot. *Jesus.* Right *there!*"

He leaned forward, forearms on the table now, standing

on tiptoes as he presented himself to Mr. Pierce. With expert deftness, Mr. Pierce lifted RC's buttocks and separated them, allowing me a glimpse of the puckered hole like a delicious treat at his center. I could see the muscles flex, could feel the tongue rimming the tight bud as if it were *my* ass upon which Mr. Pierce gorged. Softly I mimicked RC's desire-filled cries as I pulled my cock toward release. "Yes, *yes*." When the tip of his tongue disappeared into RC's hole, I whispered Mr. Pierce's real name, "Hank."

A thrill went through me. It felt so wicked, and as a result the first dribble of precum slicked my hand.

From my angle, I couldn't see RC's cock. As Mr. Pierce explored his anus with lips and tongue, RC raised one leg and set his foot on the bench where he had sat earlier. His jeans, bunched at his knees, were now pulled taut between his legs. He pushed them down, out of the way, his boxers following suit, and I finally saw the long, hard dick standing up from the dusky patch of hair at his crotch. An easy ten inches, thin, it curved to the right and made me feel impossibly inadequate. With one hand, he reached down and tugged it toward the center of his frame as if trying to corral it into place, but it had a mind of its own and continued to pull to one side. I wondered what that felt like during sex—if he fucked me, would I feel it angling one way or the other inside my ass, or would my own body be enough to tame it straight? God, I wanted to know. I wanted to crawl into the dining room, hide beneath the table, and let RC shove that thick length into my tender hole as far as it would go while Mr. Pierce took RC from behind.

I would have given anything to be brave enough to join in.

Instead I continued to watch, biting the inside of my cheek as I pleasured myself. "Hank," RC sighed, over and over again. "God," and "yes," and "Hank, *Jesus*," as if this were a religious experience for him. I knew I was close to coming, and I wasn't the one on the receiving end of Mr. Pierce's relentless ministrations. How RC didn't shoot a load, how he even managed to *stand* when my own knees wanted to buckle, was beyond me.

Finally, RC gasped, "Hank!" Louder this time, almost a command, his voice breathless. "Enough already. Just fuck me, will you?"

With a last kiss on the mole that started it all, Mr. Pierce joked, "Oh, so *now* you're ready to pay the piper."

"I want your cock," RC said, his vulgar words enflaming my blood, "in my ass, in *two* seconds, or I'm going to spaz all over the table here and you can explain to the guys next time they're over why your cards are covered in my cum."

That earned him a smack across the ass, a sound that reverberated through me and left a red mark in the shape of Mr. Pierce's hand on one round cheek. "They won't know it's yours," he muttered. He stood, unzipping his pants farther and hitching them low on his hips. His dick was still ramrod hard, but he stroked it lazily as he rubbed the fat tip up and down the cleft between RC's buttocks. "Did you bring a rubber, or do you want to ride bareback this time?"

RC straightened as he reached into the front pocket of his jeans. "What happened to your supply?"

Mr. Pierce shrugged. "I don't know. Maybe the kid got into them, who knows? Maybe we used them all up last time."

"Maybe you used them on someone else," RC teased. Extracting his hand from his pocket, he tossed a couple of coin-shaped condom packets onto the table.

Mr. Pierce reached around RC, a hand sliding under RC's shirt to smooth across his belly. His cock pressed against RC's ass, pinned between them, as Mr. Pierce leaned over the younger man. With his mouth on RC's neck, he murmured something I strained to hear. "There's no one else but you."

God. Oh, god. That phrase alone would fuel many fantasies in the days to come.

I leaned forward, my face against the louvers now, my breath hot and damp where it blew back in my face. I wanted to see everything in excruciating detail but Mr. Pierce was quick—in seconds he had the condom open and rolled onto his dick. Frustration welled in me; I wanted to replay the scene, watch it again in slow motion, see play-by-play how the lubricated condom encased his sausage-like dick. I wanted to savor the foreplay— the ease of that thick shaft between RC's tight buttocks, the filling press of cockhead to anus, the sweet pain as RC took Mr. Pierce in inch by glorious inch.

But I blinked and missed it. I saw discomfort flit over RC's features, but by the time my gaze traveled down to where their bodies melded, Mr. Pierce was already inside, his hips thrust forward, his balls hanging over the waistband of his briefs. RC's ass dimpled as he flexed, guiding Mr. Pierce deeper. Then he leaned the top half of his body down on the table, ass in the air, as Mr. Pierce found a slow, steady rhythm between them.

I renewed masturbating, timing my strokes with Mr. Pierce's. I tried to get a better look—I wanted every single moment of this night etched in my memory. I needed it, needed this, and already treasured these few stolen minutes when I was witness to something transpiring between two men that was worlds more beautiful than I had ever dared hope. I scooted closer, wanting more.

The edge of my foot struck the louvered door.

For one heart-stopping moment, Mr. Pierce seemed to freeze. RC's head was on the table now, his cheek pressed to the poker cards still lying there, and I saw his eyes swivel toward my hiding place. Every ounce of my body screamed at me to run but I couldn't move, couldn't breathe, couldn't *think*. They knew. Oh, god, they knew.

Oh, shit.

But Mr. Pierce had transcended reality—all that existed for him was his lover, the muscle encircling his cock and whatever myriad of emotions had swept him away. His movements were steady, a constant rocking that drove him into RC's ass with a gentle pounding and a faint *"Uh uh uh,"* that escaped his parted lips. So that's why Mikey made that same funny little sound when I'd heard him jerking off under the covers. Mr. Pierce leaned over RC, hands flat on the table on either side of RC's body, pushing his hips against RC's padded ass. His eyes were shut, his cheeks slack, and he was fucking not only with his dick but with every fiber of his being, giving himself wholly to the moment and the man beneath him.

After a breathless second when I was sure RC had seen me through the partially closed slats, he too gave in to their coupling. His eyes glazed over and rolled back as he moaned in pleasure. I picked up my own rhythm again, matching Mr. Pierce's, tugging myself to release not once, not twice, but three exhilarating times, each orgasm racking me silently. They felt like a strand of pearls, each one precious, pulled from me in rapid succession. My palm filled with jism; I smeared it along my length, coaxing a second ejaculation from me, and a third.

Suddenly the scene before me seemed private, too intimate, and I felt ashamed for watching. Mr. Pierce leaned over RC almost protectively, grinding his hips into his lover. RC fucked into his own hand, fondling his balls, reaching down farther to toy with Mr. Pierce's behind him as well. Together they moved toward ecstasy, each guiding the other to a climax I knew would be as mind-shattering as my own.

I leaned back against the counter to catch my breath, my sore dick now limp between my legs, my feet and legs numb from the position I'd been in for so long. Rolling my head to one side, I saw the edge of a dishtowel hanging over the counter above. I reached up, stretching, and snagged it down. The faint smell of Dawn soap wafted up from the still-damp rag, which I used to gingerly clean myself off.

In the dining room, RC's breath grew ragged. "Yes, yes," he moaned. Then, raising his voice, he cried out, "Yes! God, Hank, harder, fuck me, *harder.*"

Between clenched teeth, Mr. Pierce warned, "Shh. My son's upstairs."

"Harder," RC whispered. He pushed back against Mr. Pierce, eager to get off. "Harder, *harder.* Yeah. Oh, yeah. Yes, yes, *yes.*"

I saw Mr. Pierce's buttocks tighten inside his briefs. He thrust forward one last time, up on tiptoe now, and held that position as he threw back his head, a guttural moan rising from the back of his throat when he finally came deep within RC's ass. Mr. Pierce's orgasm triggered RC's own, and I saw a few white drops trickle down RC's wrist as he closed his hand into a fist to keep from dripping onto the floor. "God!"

Then Mr. Pierce collapsed onto RC's back. "God," he said again, his voice scratchy and hoarse with exhaustion. "You're something else, you know that? You're damn good."

RC turned his head slightly, lips pursed. "You ain't bad yourself, old man. Kiss me."

Without comment, Mr. Pierce did just that.

I blinked slowly, as if waking from a dream. A satisfying wet dream that had left me spent. I felt warm and relaxed, and if I had access to one of those packs of cigarettes left discarded on the dining room table, I would've lit up even though I'd never smoked a cigarette in my life. But I wanted to breathe in deep, hold in the moment; let it percolate within me, sear my lungs; then exhale slowly, sated. I felt as though *I* had just been the one in there, fucking, fucked. I had never found such release in masturbation before and knew, sadly, I probably never would again.

But now I knew how it could be between men, how wonderful and amazing it could be, and I looked forward to college more than ever. I wanted what I'd seen tonight, a man of my own, those kisses and that hard dick in my ass, that tight muscle encircling my cock. And I'd have it. The rest of my life spread out before me like a promise I planned to keep to myself.

All that and more.

Dazed, I pushed myself up off the floor and deposited the soiled dishcloth on the counter. With gentle fingers I tucked my now wilted member into the confines of my briefs, clammy from my own juices. I zipped up my jeans, careful to be quiet.

Hurrying to the fridge, I grabbed two bottles by their necks, then shut the door and hurried around the corner. I took the steps two at a time back to Mikey's room.

Outside Mikey's door I shifted the beers into both hands again and tapped the bottom of one bottle gently against the door. Pressing my face to the jamb, I whispered, "Mikey, it's me. I got the booze. Open up."

STEAM PUNK

Eric Del Carlo

Gay bathhouses offer anonymity, and that's why they're so popular. You don't even have to talk to anyone. You can just enjoy the bodies of men.

But a bathhouse, I've always found, is also a place of raw honesty. You are literally exposed, with nothing to hide behind except those skimpy white towels that most of the men quickly toss aside. Every inch of you will be inspected by ravenous eyes as you move from pool to steam-filled room.

The place I went to was in an old industrial building in the city's warehouse district. You wouldn't know it was a business just by looking at the grimy, stony exterior. But inside it was always jumping, every night. It was almost like a maze, with tiled passageways branching off every which way.

I paid the nameless guy at the desk and went to dump my clothes in a locker. The bathhouse staff kept a very low profile. Some men got nervous whenever anyone official was around. I could tell which ones had wives and felt sorry for them. I'd never had to lead a double life, for which I was grateful. I had been sexually active with men for the twenty years of my adulthood and had never had to apologize or lie to anybody.

My flesh was already prickling, that first low-level arousal that comes even before your cock starts to stir, when there is only anticipation. I'd been looking forward to this all day. I draped my white towel over a shoulder and padded barefoot out into the maze. At six five and with a job that kept me physically fit, I knew I cut an impressive figure. But I wasn't one of those gym-rat types who only wanted to fuck around with mirror images of themselves. I liked all kinds of men, and the bathhouse, as always, had lots of masculine possibilities on display tonight.

I passed by the main pool, where a couple dozen men were checking each other out. Some of these guys, I knew, would make a grab for the first man they saw. I wasn't that indiscriminate anymore. I needed to be genuinely attracted to a man, even an anonymous one, if I was going to screw around with him. Otherwise I could just stay home and jerk off.

I headed down a corridor. The bathhouse sprawled, and even though I knew the layout, I always felt like I could get lost here. That was part of the fun, like wandering through a wonderland of steam and male lust.

Along the way there were sauna rooms and smaller jet-pools. Guys were gathered there too. And some were doing more than just *gathering.* In one whirling pool two men grappled in the water, lips pressed together in warm kisses, hands pulling at hard cocks. A little crowd of eager onlookers sat along the edge, enjoying the show.

Farther along, a door was ajar. I looked into one of the steam rooms. Plumes of hot vapor made it look ghostly inside, but I spotted a guy on his hands and knees on the damp floor-boards that was getting his ass eaten out by a burly dude with long, slick-wet blond hair that was plastered across his broad shoulders.

Grinning, I kept heading along the rounded tunnel-like corridor. Suddenly, I heard a voice echoing off the tiles: "I told you, get the fuck away from me!"

It tripped some instinct in me, and I found myself hurrying to the corner, adrenaline starting to pump. It sounded like somebody in trouble, but when I came around the turn, I stopped short. And gaped. And caught myself just before I erupted into laughter.

The sight was so absurd. There in the middle of the corridor was a skinny, tattooed kid, pale with boot-polish black hair in a limp Mohawk. He crouched facing away from me, buck naked, and he was swinging a wet towel over his head, whipping it at a fat troll of a guy with bad skin and a leering grin. Naturally, there were no staff members on hand.

"You ain't layin' a paw on me, motherfucker, so back off!" the punk-type kid yelled.

It was pretty easy to figure out what had happened. I recognized the troll. He had boundary issues, and had been a problem before. He looked to be about twice the body mass of the stick-thin punk.

Again, I let instinct dictate my move. Without another second of hesitation, I went past the kid and blocked the corridor. "You want to keep going with this, I'll be happy to call the cops," I said to the plump predator, even though it was obvious I wasn't carrying a phone. "No means no, asshole."

He gave me an indignant look, but quickly retreated. I turned around.

The punk glared at me. He had thin, dark-red lips, and his eyes were like extinguished coals. He wanted everyone to know what a tough piece of work he was. He said, "You think I'm gonna be grateful to you now? Think you're gonna get a blow job out of this, old man? Well, you can fuckin' forget it."

He gave his towel another menacing swing. He was muscle and bone, and nothing else; a lean, lovely body, marked by at least six tattoos. He couldn't be a day over twenty.

"Fucking forget about it I will," I said amiably, smiling. Maybe I hadn't expected gratitude, but I sure didn't need this adolescent bullshit. I turned and sauntered away.

Later I heard him padding along behind me. I gave him a glance. He had the damp towel around his middle, while mine was still draped casually over my shoulder.

"You want something?" I asked.

He looked at the floor. "I'm sorry I called you *old man.*"

I laughed. "Compared to you I am so no worries. What else do you want?" Because he had to be following me for a reason.

"I..." He traced a square of tile with his big toe, still looking down. "I've never been here before. I, um, don't really know how it's s'posed to work." He raised his head. Heat had flowed into his eyes. "Can you show me?"

It was like that injection of adrenaline from a minute ago. My blood raced, and gooseflesh stood out on my arms. "Sure," I said, voice suddenly hoarse. "Let's go in here." I led him into a small nearby sauna room.

I was glad to find it empty. Not that I had a problem with anyone looking at me, but this kid was new to the scene, like he'd said. For all I knew, this was his first gay adventure.

The space was maybe twelve feet long, with a low ceiling. A wooden platform was against one wall. The air was thick with a hot dampness. I had worked hard all day, and that heat felt good. Immediately, sweat started coursing out of me, rolling down my chest. I tossed down my towel and sat on the bench.

The punk stood there, looking around. I wondered if he lived on the streets. No, I decided. Despite his thinness, he didn't look malnourished. He really was a sleek little treat.

"My name's Dale," I said. "And by telling you that, I'm breaking an unspoken rule of the bathhouse. The guys who come here like to keep it anonymous."

"I'm Curt."

"Nice to meet you, Curt. Sit down if you want. The steam feels good." I leaned back, luxuriating in the heat as it got down into my sore muscles.

He kept the towel on as he sat, but I saw him looking at my naked body. I was willing myself not to get a hard-on, despite how sexy I found Curt. I didn't want to spook him, not after he'd had that bad encounter with the troll.

After a quiet minute he said, "I like how you look." His dark eyes flashed away, and I actually saw a blush on his cheek.

It was endearing as hell. "I like how you look too. You're beautiful, Curt." My voice shook a little as I added, "I'd like to see all of you again."

He hesitated, but just for a second. Then he stood and peeled off the towel. I sat up, drinking in his body, studying him shamelessly now. His cock was rising from a nest of dark wiry curls, and that was like a signal to me. My thick cockhead rolled up my bare sweaty thigh. I watched him watching me.

"I never done this before!" he blurted. His shallow chest was rising and falling. I could see each one of his ribs. "I mean, I'm no virgin. I messed around with guys before, but it's always been with some ugly shithead or somebody who just wants to get himself off and leaves me hanging—"

I was surprised to see tears spring into his eyes. I stood and stepped toward him, moved. I folded him into my arms. His narrow body felt good against mine, but this contact was more than sexual. Curt had a rough time of it—bad sex partners, unlucky situations.

"It's okay," I told him, stroking his damp un-gelled Mohawk. His face was nuzzled against my neck, his arms holding me tight. I felt his still-hardening cock against my leg.

His lips brushed my throat as the steam continued to rise all around us. "I figured if I came to a place like this," I heard him murmur, "maybe I'd find somebody, who, y'know..."

I could have told him he *had* found someone that would treat him right, but words were cheap.

Slipping a knuckle under his chin to gently tilt back his head, I bent to press my lips against his. I felt his body stiffen. He returned my kiss. I didn't rush it; I was too busy savoring.

Our kisses deepened, at which point he boldly thrust his tongue into my mouth. It was luscious. His fingers dug into my back. His cock surged into full hardness. He was rubbing against my leg. I was practically licking his tonsils as I caressed his back with my other hand, tracing his spine down to the taut halves of his ass.

Curt moaned into my mouth. He pushed against me but not to shove me away. Together we stumbled toward the broad wood bench, still kissing crazily. He had a wiry strength to him, with enough muscle in that slim body to force me down onto the platform. It occurred to me how lucky that bad-skinned troll from before was. If he'd tried anything serious, Curt probably would have put out his lights.

I was lying back now, the damp wood warm underneath me. Sweat streamed into my eyes. Curt, with a flushed face, collapsed on top of me. I opened my arms as he laid his hard, lithe body on mine. We kissed again. He writhed, grinding his cock against mine, which sent pleasure through my slick body. I groped his flexing ass again, pressing a finger against his asshole.

A few strands of his dyed black Mohawk had fallen over his eyes. Beads of sweat dripped down the shaved sides of his skull. Both his ears were pierced with lots of studs. As he continued to wriggle his slippery body on top of mine, I realized one of his nipples was pierced.

I wondered about the sex he'd had with those other guys; if there'd been time for niceties like this. Nobody had ever come close to *making love* to Curt, I felt sure.

He sucked my nipples, grinning between licks. Even as my excitement rose and my back arched under me, I kept an eye on his sweet young face. Bliss washed over his features. He caught me with his teeth, but he was gentle about it, following instincts he probably didn't know he had. Then he traded off to my left nip.

"I gotta have your cock in my mouth!" he said.

I grinned. "Yeah. Suck it. Please." My heart was thudding in my chest.

I continued to watch him as he kissed and nibbled his way down my body. My cock was straining, desperate for the touch of his moist lips. He settled between my legs, his hard bony shoulders pressing apart my thighs. His shapely ass pointed up in the air as he lowered his mouth.

Stray hairs tickled my belly as his fingers took hold of my shaft at its thick base. His other hand closed lightly around my balls. Resting on his elbows, he gave my cockhead a tentative lick. *Maybe he won't like it*, I thought. *Maybe this will remind him of bad past experiences.* But I was being silly. Curt's tongue went swirling wildly over my fat plum, and my whole body squirmed with pleasure.

My nipples ached from the thorough sucking he'd given them. My balls stirred in his delicate grip. I was mesmerized by the sight of Curt's lips around the head of my cock, his mouth dropping inch by inch down my veined piece. He swallowed me to my balls. My head thumped back down on the bench. My eyes were closed to the intense sexual joy.

His tongue worked me over. When his head rose, I cried out loud when he dropped his mouth again. He maintained a perfect suction as he started a bobbing rhythm on me. Whatever else he'd taken away from his previous sexual escapades, he'd sure learned how to suck a cock!

Red flashes were going off on the backs of my eyelids. Steam coated me, and sweat continued to roll off my body. The heat of the sauna was nothing compared to the seething, living warmth of Curt's talented mouth. Carnal energy radiated outward from my cock, spreading to every part of me. My limbs tingled. My toes bunched. I was thrusting up with every downward plunge he made. My hips were trying to lift up from the platform. Curt kept a grip on me with his hands and mouth.

I let loose a wail. My hands flailed at my sides. Curt's speed increased. Finally I had to see his beautiful face, even as my orgasm started to overtake me.

I lifted my head, just as my balls tightened and my hot, heavy juice started to fly. Curt, who could feel it on its way, wrenched his mouth off me. My cum shot over his shoulder, a few pearly flecks dotting the shaved side of his head. He grabbed my shaft and started pumping furiously. Pleasure ripped through my body.

Curt was grinning again, watching the white globs land. He jerked me through my last few quivering spasms, then let go of my softening cock. I was panting, barely able to get a breath, but I felt wonderful. It had been a *cum* to remember. Even the afterglow felt great.

I wiped my damp face with a damp palm, unsure where I'd tossed my towel. But when I looked at Curt again, he'd stopped grinning. In fact, he'd shrunk away from me on the bench, an uncertain look on his face.

Uneasiness grabbed me, but then I realized. He was afraid I was going to ditch him now that I'd gotten off. I silently cursed the assholes who'd been so uncaring with him. I sat up and reached out my hand.

"Come here," I said.

He gave me his hand, and I pulled him to me, closing my arms over him again. I smelled my cum on him. I kissed his temple, feeling a vein beating there.

"That was fantastic," I murmured. "Now let me do the same for you."

He sat up on the wood bench, feet planted on the ground and legs spread. I knelt on the floor, the soggy boards giving a little under my knees. Curt's cock reared up before me, the crown swollen, the shaft veiny. He had a tattoo on either hip, I saw. One was an Oriental character, the other a flaming skull. I took hold of his meat, feeling his pulse beat urgently. I had a last look up through the steam, seeing him gazing down at me, mouth open and eyes wide. He wanted it so bad.

I gave it to him.

When I licked his cockhead with my tongue, his knees clamped my shoulders. I felt the coiled strength of him. I loved the texture of his knob and rolled my lips over it until he let out a needy groan. I plunged down his staff, taking him all the way in a single swallow.

I buried my nose in his damp, dark curls, inhaling his scent. I took his cock down my throat, holding it there. My tongue continued to strum his shaft. I lifted my head, keeping my lips sealed around him, squeezing him. I knew my talents as a cocksucker, and I wanted to share everything I had with Curt.

As I started bobbing up and down on him, his strong narrow

body jerked. His ass fidgeted on the wood, and his bony knees gripped my shoulders harder, like a vise. He moaned louder. I kept up a deliberate speed, wanting him to enjoy the experience.

Pretty soon he let me know how much he was liking it: "That's so fuckin' good! I can't believe how good you suck!"

The corners of my stretched-out mouth turned up in a secret smile as I continued to blow him. But he deserved the full benefit of the experience. I wriggled my free hand beneath his sweat-slick ass, finding his hole and slipping a fingertip up into him. He just about shrieked with pleasure. His hands were suddenly raking through my hair. His hips rose. He was face-fucking me.

I probed his ass deeper, wiggling my finger up to the knuckle. I felt his sweet, tight passage clamping around my digit. He pulled harder at my hair. He was shouting more things now, but I couldn't hear. Blood roared in my ears. I sucked him faster, mouth slurping, everything a blur of flesh and steam.

My finger was all the way up into him when I felt his cock start to spasm. Reluctantly I pulled my mouth off him as he began to shoot. Hot droplets spattered my shoulder, and I smelled the beautiful salty tang. His ass muscles clenched as spurt after spurt jerked from his cock.

He let go of my hair. I sat back on my haunches, looking up at him. He lay back limp and spent, a look of satisfaction on his pale face. He knew what it was all about, I thought, and I was happy for him. I was glad no one had interrupted us. That got me thinking that it might be nice to see Curt outside the bath-house, someplace private. But that could wait.

Smiling, he reached down for me, and I climbed up to nestle with him again, my new steamy punk lover.

THE CHICKEN COOP

David Holly

Farmer Cutler was the sternest, tightest and strictest native of Tillamook County. His word was the way it was, and his opinions, prejudices and pruderies seemed to have been handed down from on high. There was Farmer Cutler, Mrs. Farmer Cutler and their son Rupert Cutler. Rupert was my age, and the most obnoxious boy in the whole county. If you've ever heard the expression "holier than thou," then you have an accurate picture of Rupert and his parents.

No one in his right mind would want to shovel shit for Farmer Cutler. So why was I spending the summer after my high school graduation working as his farmhand? Well, you see, the Cutlers attended our church, and my father—in a misguided outpouring of Christian charity—had volunteered my services.

"Since Chad graduated high school, he hasn't lifted a finger except to tap his video game console. Pay him what you will. He'll be at your farm at seven tomorrow morning."

"Five in the morning would be better." Farmer Cutler said. "I'll get him started with the milking."

By the morning of the fifth day, I was frazzled. Not to mention, I had gone four days without even getting a chance to jerk off. Farmer Cutler was always around, and if he wasn't, Mrs. Farmer Cutler or Rupert were. Rupert was the worst. He would sit and read Bible verses at me while I cleaned up after the cows. Just when I was feeling lowest, Farmer Cutler told me that he was getting new birds next week, so I had to clean out the chicken coop.

The chicken coop was constructed on three levels. There was a roosting area, which was thick with ancient chicken shit and heaven-only-knew-what, a raised catwalk around the interior of the coop, and the bottom floor with the rows of egg boxes. I leaned against the railing, surveyed the mess and nearly cried. Then a rebellious thought struck me. I suddenly realized I had been scratching the head of my cock through my jeans while I was standing lost in thought. What if I jerked off in Farmer Cutler's chicken coop?

My cock was more than half hard already. Standing on the catwalk with my ass pressed against the railing, I pushed down my jeans and briefs and fingered my cock. It hardened completely in an instant. I massaged my cockhead between my forefinger and thumb, played with it and wrung it for a few seconds. Then I spit into my hand and slicked my cock. I rubbed the spit over my dickhead and down the shaft. Adding more spit, I stroked my shaft slowly. Eighteen years old multiplied by four days of unwilling chastity was sure to equal a shuddering orgasm and a massive ejaculation. I tried to stroke even slower, but the merest touch of thumb and forefinger on the head of my cock threatened to commit me to a rapid climax.

Just as I decided to finish and let fly, the chicken coop door rattled. I pulled my briefs over my erection and tried to fasten my jeans. My heart thundered, while my face both cooked and chilled. Making my way around the catwalk, I pushed open the door. I saw nothing but the Holsteins grazing in the sunny pasture. I stuck my head out and even looked around the door. No one.

My cock had completely deflated by then, but it took no time at all to bring it back to full rigidity. My hands were slick with my spit, and I was thumbing the head of my cock with one while I was jerking the shaft with the other. I could feel the first tingles that signaled oncoming orgasm when the door rattled again. Distracted, I stopped masturbating, halting my orgasm before it started. Still I had both hands on my spit-slick cock when the door swung wide open and Rupert leaped in as if he had been goosed. He raised a hand and pointed directly at my cock.

"Have no fellowship with the unfruitful works of darkness." Rupert was blowing Ephesians at me, while he pulled the chicken-coop door shut behind him.

I turned toward him, rubbing my cock ever so slowly and meaningfully. "Oh, Rupert, no man ever yet hated his own flesh; but nourisheth and cherisheth it," I quoted, squirting a dose of Ephesians back his way. I expected him to flee, to run crying for his daddy who would condemn my soul to everlasting torment before notifying my parents and the rest of the church that I was an unclean, idolatrous disciple of Onan.

To my shock, Rupert pushed close to me at the rail, stripped off his trousers and gripped his cock. "Ah, Chad," he gasped. "Do it this way—like you're wringing out a washcloth." So saying, he spit into his hands and using both, he wrung his cock in two directions. "Do it gently," he warned. "You won't believe how hard you'll squirt."

I tried his technique, taking care not to break my cock in the process. I was wringing the head of my dick harder than I twisted the shaft, and I felt the tingles start again. "I'm going to come fast."

"You started before me," Rupert said rather accusingly, as if I should have invited him. "Tell you what: let's do each other." He pushed my hands aside and gripped my cock with a back-handed grab.

Maybe Rupert wasn't so "holier than thou" after all. Whatever he was doing to me, it wasn't a grip I could refuse. Throwing caution to the birds, I slicked my hand with my spit, grabbed on to his cock and jerked him hard. I squeezed the head of his dick, pressing my thumb down hard on his pisshole.

The tingles in my cock turned into an anguished prickling. The prickles spiked into sharp barbs of pleasure that quivered my dick and contracted and dilated my asshole. My cum spurted along Rupert's arm, and as my cum touched his skin, he crashed into full orgasm himself.

"Chad, that's fuckin' good," he gasped, as I jacked him off, all the while pressing my thumb against his pisshole to maximize his pleasure. His cum exploded around my thumb, and I used his own semen to jack him harder.

After we finished, we cleaned up with some of the rags and water I had brought to wash away the shit left by chickens who had probably gotten eaten a decade earlier. We were both pretty much a mess, considering the volume of spit and cum we'd expelled, but we managed to get rid of most of the evidence.

For a few minutes, we could only grin rather stupidly at each other. I didn't know what to say; however, Rupert finally worked up the nerve to ask whether I'd still be working in the chicken coop the next day.

"It's a four-day job, at least, Rupert."

"How about I meet you here tomorrow, Chad?"

And so we jerked each other off in the chicken coop every afternoon—until the day the goddamned poultry arrived.

A PORT IN THE STORM

Dilo Keith

I answered the phone at the front desk and a deep, sexy voice said, "I'm looking for Eliot Silverman."

"Speaking," I said. "How may I help you?"

"I heard that you'll print anything I want on a business card and that I should ask for you."

"Almost anything. What did you have in mind?"

It turned out he wanted a photograph of his cock—bold, but not very original. He thought it would leave an impression at the clubs he frequented. I offered suggestions for effective lighting and tasteful poses to make it more than just another boring cock shot. Most people do that sort of thing on home printers, badly. Fortunately for me, others appreciate the quality I offer. Competing with the numerous digital arts and services providers meant doing something different for our customers, and word was getting around about our "special" offerings.

Today, however, I would have preferred something that didn't remind me of other people fucking. Michael and I had had next to no sex for over a week, due to his working late every night and being out of town on business the past weekend. Jamie, Michael's part-time submissive and the third in our ongoing threesome, had also been unavailable. Michael and I had managed a quick blow job here and there, but that wasn't going to help now even if I'd had the chance. I wanted Michael to walk in the door and bend me over the arm of our leather couch, taking time only to free his cock. I'd lube my ass before he arrived. I could jerk off as soon as I got home—or maybe before I left work—so I could go slowly, worshipping his body first, savoring all the tastes and smells I hadn't been able to enjoy lately.

In reality, all I had was Michael saying something about a chance of getting home earlier tonight, but I suspected he'd stay if there was any work left. A little persuasion might help, though I was reluctant to disturb him with my selfish desires. *Taking a break will make him more productive, right?* During the drive home, I thought about what I might say.

In the privacy of our living room, for the third time in an hour, I had my finger on the key for his number. I finally pressed it, hoping I'd catch him on a break.

"Perfect timing," Michael said. "I'm eating the meatloaf Jamie left."

Fuck, that means he's staying. "At least you're taking care of yourself, but..." *Seems he's not even trying to get home.*

"But what?" he prompted.

"What happened to finishing early tonight?"

"It's not like I have a choice."

"But you said—"

Michael cut me off. "Don't whine or I'll make time to find that paddle you hate when I finally get there, even if you're asleep."

He's not serious—just cranky about working. "Isn't it my turn to top?" I honestly didn't know—we hadn't planned anything—but it was a way to turn the conversation to sex.

"Not until I say it is. Besides, if that's what you want, Jamie will be there soon. You know he'll do anything you say."

That was true. When Michael first brought home that sweet young thing—literally half his age—I hadn't dreamed we'd end up with such a delightfully kinky, pliant and obedient sub who wasn't fazed by a dom who switched once in a while.

"I don't want to top Jamie now." I fondled the growing bulge behind my zipper. "I actually don't want to top you, not tonight. What I want is to lick and suck you all over before I sit on your cock. I'll lower myself slowly, inch by inch, squeezing and—"

"Stop that."

Cranky and *horny.*

He continued, "I need to finish here. What's gotten into you?"

"Nothing, for over a week now."

Michael chuckled. "I guess I set myself up for that. You're not the only one who's gone a week without a proper fuck. Did something happen today?"

"It could have been all the work I've been doing on the Three-H site."

"The what?"

"Hot, Hairy and Hung. I'm calling it that until Greg comes up with a name. I worked on the photo gallery today. Eight pages of steamy manliness. It's coming together rather nicely. Wish we were."

"Me too, but I need another couple of hours here, at least. Try to behave, El."

"Sorry to be a pest."

"It's okay. I miss you too," Michael said, sounding like he

meant it rather than simply being nice to his horny partner.

"See you when you get here." *And I'll keep something hot for you.*

I unbuttoned my jeans and reached for the zipper, but stopped when I heard the front door unlock. Not that Jamie would find the sight of my hands on my dick unusual—he'd be ready to help. In fact, he might turn out to be useful.

I hurried to meet Jamie in the foyer, where he stood with a bag of groceries in each hand. He hadn't yet closed the door, so I took care of that before pouncing.

"Great to see you! Let me help you with that. Did you have a nice day?" I ignored his incredulous stare and tugged at his coat after setting his bags on the floor.

He managed to get out, "Are you okay, El? I mean, Sir."

I was more interested in nuzzling his neck than enforcing protocol. "Mmm, you smell good." He was sweaty, but not dirty. I licked his warm skin from neckline to ear before going back to getting him out of his coat, which I dropped where he stood. "You can get that later. Does any of this have to go in the fridge?"

"Yes, Sir, the salmon and yogurt."

"Let's go." I grabbed the cold items and took Jamie's hand.

"What's going on?" Jamie asked with a hint of nervousness as I pulled him across the room.

"You're helping me in the kitchen."

"With what?"

"Michael said he'd be late again, still working on that big project. We haven't fucked all week."

He breathed a faint sigh of relief as he discovered that there was sex rather than a problem or a pile of dirty dishes waiting for him. "I live to serve, Sir, and no task is too onerous."

"Smartass."

"One thing, though," Jamie said, "Michael wants me to install and configure some new programs. Sorry."

"Now?" *Please say no.* "When did he call?" I stuffed the bag of cold food into the fridge as I spoke.

"He texted me an hour ago."

"Oh, before he...never mind. Did he say when he needed it?"

"He wasn't specific, Sir, but I think he meant I should do it when I got here. Something about using it later."

I wonder if Michael forgot that when he recommended having my way with our boy toy. "His 'later' is going to be hours from now. If you don't think he meant immediately, I want you. We'll be quick, and you'll have time to do it."

"He usually tells me when he has a specific time in mind. I'm all yours."

"Excellent." I reached for Jamie's belt and started to unbuckle it. "You can undress yourself." I let go. "Leave the shirt on." He could have simply opened his fly, something I'd find hot if he were a real top, but he wasn't. Plus I didn't want to get lube or any other mess on his clothes. I cleared a space on the table and opened a nearby drawer to find what we needed.

Once stripped from the waist down, Jamie asked, "Where do you want me?"

He stood there looking so eager to submit to my whims. His slender body and small stature appealed to Michael more than they did to me. I prefer a man with a little more bulk and muscle, someone closer to my and Michael's build, but Jamie had a charming cuteness that worked well. He was dark blond like Michael, which I liked—even though there wasn't enough hair in my opinion, due to a combination of nature and Michael's grooming instructions—with a soft dusting of hair on his lightly muscled thighs. More important at the moment was what resided where those thighs met. Above a lovely pair of low-hanging balls was the part I wanted—big, beautiful, half-hard, and, for the moment, all mine. Jamie's uncut cock was long and slender (but not too slender!) like the rest of him, and often located halfway down my throat after Michael and I tied him up. I tossed the lube and strip of condoms onto the table. "In my ass, after you get me ready." I shoved my briefs and khakis down to my shoes.

"Oh."

Jamie's reluctant tone stopped me. I turned in his direction and saw a man without the happy look of someone about to bury his cock in a willing ass. "What's wrong? You've fucked me before. I recall you have a talent for it."

Jamie had seen Michael fuck me numerous times and thankfully didn't subscribe to the notion that doms shouldn't get fucked. We didn't usually do it in play scenes, but I was on the bottom for most of the vanilla sex Michael and I had in Jamie's presence. About a month ago, Michael had ordered Jamie to fuck me while he watched. Jamie was surprisingly attuned to what I liked and needed little direction from either me or Michael. He had me squirming around his fingers and ready to beg for his cock. I was spared from that un-domly display by Michael's order to "get on with it." I didn't expect that Jamie wouldn't be thrilled by a repeat performance.

"I'm surprised, Sir. And, um, Sir…"

"What?" I asked, a little curtly. *I just want a simple fuck.*

"I'm not sure what you…um…"

El, you idiot, Jamie wants to please you. He was following Michael's orders before—we hadn't been alone like this. "Don't worry about it. I just want to get fucked, nothing fancy."

I pressed the lube into Jamie's hand and positioned myself on the kitchen table, feet on the floor and chest on the surface. Not the most comfortable spot, but all I cared about was having my ass within reach of the dick behind me.

Jamie's lubed finger encountered little resistance from my body. "You're right about being quick. I think you can take two already."

"Just do it. I trust you. No rules except not making me wait."

Jamie worked his fingers all the way in, rotating them to stroke my prostate exquisitely. He'd definitely been paying attention.

"Oh, that's it. More."

"More this?" He prodded the sensitive nub. "Or more fingers?"

It almost sounded like he was teasing me, an encouraging sign. "More of everything except questions."

Jamie didn't need to ask if "everything" included his tongue in my ass. Of course it did. He used it like a warm, wet finger to open me even more. It wasn't long before his swollen cock was covered, lubed and pressing against my not-so-patiently awaiting hole where Jamie paused for my approval.

"Now!"

Jamie obeyed, plunging fully inside me with a single thrust.

"Fuck, yeah," we gasped in stereo.

After a few slow strokes, Jamie asked, "How do you want it, *Sir*?" He emphasized the last word with both his voice and a deep thrust.

"Fast. Hard. Like Michael does it. Oh yeah, that's it..." There was no hint of uncertainty now, which was fortunate as I really wasn't in the frame of mind to coax or instruct him.

Jamie didn't mimic the way Michael usually held me down; instead he leaned on the table for balance as he wordlessly pounded away. He did such a superb job on my prostate that I almost blew my load from that alone. Close, but not enough.

"Touch me," I commanded in a stern whisper. With little break in rhythm, Jamie reached around to jerk me off. I soon rewarded his efforts with a handful of pulsing cock and what was certainly a double helping of master cream. My throbbing hole clamped down around his shaft, hastening his orgasm. He stayed deep inside me, his smooth crotch jammed against my sweaty ass while his balls emptied themselves. Jamie collapsed on my back and we lay there motionless, apart from the heaving of our chests with ragged breaths, until he pushed himself up.

"S'okay," I said. "Stay."

I heard a throat clearing behind us and we both twisted around, somehow doing so with Jamie's dick still inside me. Michael stood in the doorway holding Jamie's coat and the shopping bag I'd left beside it.

In the most cheerful tone I could muster, I said, "Hi honey, welcome home. I didn't hear you come in. We missed you."

"I can see that." He hung Jamie's coat on a chair and deposited the food on the counter.

Other than his warranted sarcasm, he gave no hint of reaction, positive or negative, so I forged on. "Aren't you home early? Or did we lose track of time?"

Jamie backed out of my ass, grabbed a napkin from the table for the condom and silently knelt before Michael in his ritual greeting.

Michael's hand on my shoulder thwarted my attempt to stand. "Stay there." The swat on my butt left no doubt that he was talking to me. "You sounded so hot on the phone, I decided to come home. I thought I'd work here after seeing to you."

"Oh," I said. *I should probably apologize, but it was Michael who had said I should play with Jamie, even if he hadn't meant it this way.* Before I could say anything, Michael addressed Jamie.

"Does this mean you're finished with my computer?"

"No, Sir. I'm sorry."

"Explain why you weren't doing what I said."

"Sir, when Eliot asked if you had meant immediately, it occurred to me I didn't really know. He said you were going to be late, so a small delay seemed okay. I'd say I made the wrong choice, Sir."

"So would I, although it wasn't outright disobedience and you still have time. Bring me the paddle Eliot keeps in his desk drawer." Michael turned to me and said, "Stand up, but don't go anywhere." He was clearly in dom mode, which was unexpected, but not surprising.

Jamie returned with the paddle and Michael used it to tap the spot I had just vacated, a crystal-clear order. The chosen implement was a scaled-down version of a fraternity paddle—long and narrow, with holes to increase the intensity of the sting. In other words, it could hurt like hell. Its more common use was in the naughty schoolboy scenes I did with Jamie bent over my desk, but I'd been on the receiving end when Jamie wasn't around.

Michael laid into Jamie's ass harder than I would have for something trivial, even though Jamie's quite the pain slut. He took the first stroke silently, but clenched his ass in his usual sexy way for just a moment before relaxing to receive the second one. My cock stirred a little at the sight.

Michael stopped after only two, suggesting that it was merely a symbolic reminder, and told him, "This would be a good time to take care of my computer. Put on your pants first. Just so it's perfectly clear, I mean immediately, except that you may stop in the bathroom or get a drink of water if you need to. I imagine you lost some fluid recently."

Jamie thanked him and scurried away.

I asked Michael, "Are you mad?"

"Jamie knows not to let you interfere with one of my orders. I assumed *you* knew that."

He was still holding the paddle—not a reassuring sign. "I do. I honestly wasn't sure you meant immediately, without doing anything else first. I wouldn't have tried to talk him out of a direct order. I just wanted—"

"I know what you wanted." He pulled me toward the table where I knew to arrange myself in the position Jamie had just demonstrated. "I'm not angry. I'm not even upset. But I still get to punish you." He slid the paddle across my ass while he spoke.

"This is for encouraging Jamie to interpret my order in a way that suited you and your hungry asshole. It's also for being such a slut you couldn't wait after sounding so hot on the phone. Did you consider that I might want you ready for me?"

"No, Sir. I'm sorry, Sir." I braced myself. After coming, I wasn't in the mood to enjoy pain. The severity of Jamie's "punishment" didn't bode well for my ass.

"Ow! Fuck!" The first stroke was harder than Jamie's, or so it seemed.

"A lot of fuss over a little paddling," he teased. "Try to take the next ones with some composure."

A little! And "ones"? "How many, Sir?" I asked.

"As many as I think you deserve, plus one for swearing during punishment."

He usually reserved the no-warm-up beating for more intense scenes—real offenses or a display of submission. Not being upset with me now, that probably meant only a few—a sadist's idea of foreplay, another thing we hadn't done for over a week. Hoping I was right, I braced myself and thought about getting his cock when he finished.

He laid four more blazing strokes across my ass. Foreplay or not, those fuckers hurt. Then, instead of mounting me, he told me to stand. *Have I misread his feelings? Is he annoyed?*

"I'm sorry," I offered again.

"I believe you. But you're still a slut. You couldn't wait for my cock. Or maybe you were in the mood for a bigger one."

Okay, he's just toying with me. "Jamie's not that much bigger, Sir."

He slapped my face, once, just hard enough for my cock to like it.

"Try again."

"I missed you so much I wasn't thinking."

Michael slapped my other cheek. "Better, but not quite right."

My cock told me to cut the cute remarks and say whatever would get us fucked again. "I probably don't deserve your cock now, but I hope you'll allow me a chance to please you."

"That will do." His firm hand on my shoulder prompted me to kneel. He opened his fly and said, "Get it wet and harder."

While a bit shorter than Jamie's, Michael's cock has a very satisfying heft, even semierect. I always love the way it feels on my tongue, and I was no longer in a huge rush for it to be elsewhere. Michael, however, was. He silently guided me back to the table and pressed his wet cock against my asshole.

"Don't move."

I obediently froze as Michael sank balls-deep inside me. He groaned in both relief from pent-up tension and an effort to avoid coming too quickly. The iron grip on my hips was for controlling himself, not me. After a few steadying breaths he said, "I can't tell you how glad I am Jamie got you ready."

"Then *show* me, Sir."

And he did.

STICKS AND STONES

Gregory L. Norris

Let's be clear about one thing: the dude was a fucking idiot. A tool, a moron, a real *dick*. If not for his dick, I'd call him a waste of oxygen. I'd call him worse. He'd hurled plenty of insults my way during our respective youth growing up in a lousy little hellhole called Salem. I left; he stayed. I came back for a new job and rented the downstairs apartment of a house on Height Street, unaware that my path was about to again cross that of Donald Lavallee, my former high-school nemesis, the fucking lowlife.

Boxes sat stacked in minor mountain ranges around the two-bedroom apartment. None of my furniture save the bed was where it belonged, and even that was out of alignment, pushed at an angle beneath the windows. It was the first morning following the move; a day with a heat index just this side of the planet Mercury broke bright and muggy. I was sore, exhausted, *hot*. The box fan launched warm air at my naked back, offering only mild relief. My first task of the morning after a tall iced coffee would be to install the air conditioner in the bedroom window. If I could find the thing.

I rolled over, the bed familiar, though nothing else was. Then I remembered my new surroundings: back in the town of Salem after twelve years away. The money at the new job was great, the rent on Height Street fairly cheap. But my hatred for this town had built over the years. Not even a full day and I was ready to leave.

I reached down, found my dick erect and was thinking about giving it a tug when I caught a flash of motion beyond the bedroom windows, bald of curtains and facing the house's backyard. I sat up in time to see a lone figure plodding toward the Dumpster. A man. The image of his spine drew all the moisture from my mouth and made my already-hard cock pulse in my boxers.

He was carrying a garbage bag. He lifted the Dumpster's lid, exposing lush pit fur, and tossed in the bag. The loud clank of bottles shattered the morning's relative calm, heavy like thunder in the muggy air. Some disconnected register in my thoughts shamed the dude for not recycling while another guessed those empties had once contained beer. The rest absorbed the physique of the man outside my windows.

He had the torso of an athlete, his hips slender, lacking handles. Shapely butt was showcased to perfection in an old pair of khaki pants that hung off those hips minus a belt, flashing plenty of elastic waistband and a few inches of dark cotton underwear. He wasn't wearing a shirt. Freckled shoulders, plenty of ink on arm muscles: I couldn't tell the designs from my position and his present angle. Chestnut hair in a jock's cut, neat on the nape of the neck and around the ears. The most telling facet of the man's image were the socks on his big, flat feet: formerly white, now a degree dirtier, because he hadn't bothered to slide his sweaty dogs into shoes en route to getting rid of the evidence of the previous night's booze fest, which I'd clearly slept through in my exhaustion.

I hoped loud parties weren't going to be a regular occurrence here. I'd signed a yearlong lease. At least I could look forward to regular cheap thrills from my upstairs neighbor, who looked great from the back and as if he clearly had pretty much given up to the point he couldn't be bothered to slide his clodhoppers into an old pair of sneakers for the hundred or so steps to the Dumpster. Blue-collar white trash. The sort of bonehead I routinely jerk my dick over and enjoy the occasional blow-and-go with.

Orange August light infused the morning, painting the world in an impression of flames. I drew in a deep breath, smelled the lush green fragrance of newly mowed lawns and figured his body was equally magical in its male, funky scent up close. His mission accomplished, he turned and started back toward the door to the front hallway that joined our two apartments. I noticed the cancer stick dangling from lips wreathed in day-old scruff before gravity and lust dragged my eyes down a sculpted chest with a patch of chestnut hair at the top center and a line of fur cutting down the middle of a sculpted abdomen. Nice bulge at the crotch. A big toe poked through a hole in one dirty sock. En route back up to the dude's face, I identified the ink: an Iron Cross, a naked woman, a human skull, barbed wire.

Higher: hairy throat, chin and cheeks. Generic handsomeness, the hard kind you see on millions of men. Clearly, my upstairs neighbor was one of those small-town tough guys who smoke cigarettes, drink too much beer and lounge around shirtless on hot summer days. He blew another noxious puff of gray. When the toxic cloud dispersed, I noticed something else about the dude as he reached down and scratched his balls through his pants without worry or apology, clueless that I was watching.

"Holy fuck," I gasped.

I knew that dick. He was my greatest tormenter, my worst enemy from a decade-plus gone by. I had moved into the apartment beneath the one he rented.

"Donald Lavallee," I said, my voice barely above a whisper.

A look at the upstairs tenant's mailbox in the front hallway confirmed it. The same fucker who'd made my life miserable starting in junior high was walking around over my head, his big, smelly feet squeaking around on the floorboards, stinking up the place. I was as horrified as I was turned on. Little as I wanted to admit it, the fuck-wad who used to call me "cocksucker," "cum breath," and a slew of other slurs, most involving my presumed penchant for gobbling dick and guzzling buckets of skeet, looked better than fine.

I jerked off fantasizing about sucking on the long, lanky dick that lurked over sweaty balls in his underwear and khakis, and chuckled at the irony after I came. Back in Salem; and nothing much had changed except twelve years of birthdays and mailing addresses.

I set about unpacking, installed the air conditioner and put up curtains. I didn't know how long I'd manage to escape Donald's notice but suspected it wouldn't be long.

Two days later, I pulled into our shared driveway to see a shitty pickup truck more rust than actual metal parked in my assigned spot beside the wreck of an old blue four-door that hadn't moved since my arrival. I pulled my car onto the lawn and got out. Fucking inconsiderate ape upstairs and his fellow primate friends I thought, too tired to do more than gripe to myself.

As I worked the key into my front door's lock, the loud clomp of footsteps thundered down the staircase. I got into my new apartment in time to avoid any visual contact. A pair of male tenor voices grunted in the front hallway. I watched from the window as Don and another dude not much higher up the evolutionary ladder said their good-byes in the driveway, lit cigarettes clamped between teeth. Don wore his T-shirt draped over one shoulder. The vision of that perfect torso and inked sleeve drained the last of the moisture from my mouth. So, too, did the fact that he was barefoot.

The other dude got into his truck and started the engine. The earth quaked. The truck pulled out. I turned from the window, unknotted my tie. I was contemplating a cold diet soda when a series of sharp knocks sounded on the front door. My pulse galloped. There was no avoiding the reunion any longer.

Getting to the door seemed far longer than the actual few seconds and steps. Donald Lavallee stood on the other side, the foul stink of cigarette smoke announcing him ahead of the big reveal.

"Yo," he said. Fucking idiot.

I gave him a tip of my chin, that universal greeting between males, the human equivalent of a deep sniff around the asshole so happily explored by other mammals.

"Yeah, just wanted to let you know that my buddy's out of your parking spot."

"Great," I said, my mouth operating separately from my consciousness, the rest of me focused totally on the image of the man at my open door: all man, an amazing primitive specimen despite the putrid cigarette smoke and his lack of gray matter. I absorbed the vision of his ripped musculature, the way Donald's scant clothes loved his body, caught the scent of his sweaty armpits between toxic, ashy ribbons.

"I'm Don," he said. "Live upstairs."

He gestured toward the staircase with a tip of his skull. And then he extended his hand. The same hand he used to jerk his dick, to scratch his low-swinging nuts and hairy ass, to pick at the funky stink between his toes, those incredible bare toes drifting in and out of focus at the periphery of my line of sight. The same hand that had delivered so much misery during my teen years, on courtyards and in locker rooms.

"I know who the fuck you are, goat-boy," I growled.

"Huh?"

The world plunged beneath a filter of red. Balling my fist, I swung, clocking the handsome moron on his chin hard enough to launch the cigarette from his mouth and knocking him onto his dumb ass.

What felt like a very long time later, I blinked the red out of my eyes and shook out my hand. Donny-boy scrambled back to his feet and massaged his jaw.

"What the fuck?"

I knew he wouldn't call the cops. Not my old pal Don's style. What I didn't factor into the knock to his noggin was that one punch wasn't likely going to take him out of the fight. Don Lavallee was an animal. An injured one now, thus far more dangerous.

He sprang at me, striking with enough force to tip me over. The room spun. Don scrambled on top, and his face—his rage only enhancing its handsomeness—got close to mine.

"What's your fucking problem?" he barked, spraying spittle.

"You are, ball-sac!"

I shoved. Don landed beneath me. For a brief and thrilling instant while our dicks mashed together, I assumed the Top Dawg position.

"A lot has changed since high school, Donny-boy," I said, a smile I imagined looking quite mad blooming on my expression. "I'm not so easy a target anymore."

My dick grinned as well, trapped in my dress pants and

pinned at an awkward angle in my boxers. I grew aware of its hardness, pressed against his, right as recognition dawned in my adversary's pale blue eyes.

"Cargill?" he huffed. "*Cocksucker Cargill?*"

I drew back, ready to clock the fucker again, the scent of his body infusing my shallow sips of breath with ever more hypnotic power. But lightning-fast, Don flipped me back onto my spine and electricity rushed through my cells, launched from my dick as it rubbed against his thickness.

"Fucking Cargill," Don chuckled. "Nothing's changed— you're still some jizz-gulping cock-smoocher. Only older and probably better at it."

Don cuffed my wrists against the floor. I struggled, humped upward, saw stars as our cocks collided. The position put his sweaty armpits close over my face. Their ripeness filled my lungs. The manly stink of his feet drifted up and into the mix, too. I wanted to beat the fuck out of him. I wanted him to fuck me one iota more.

A slippery grin broke across my old and current enemy's mouth. "Cargill, what the fuck are you doing here?"

"Paying my rent on time, moron," I said. "I'm shocked that you don't still live in your mom's basement."

"My mother don't have no basement."

"Oh yeah, that's right—because her house is on wheels."

Don made a face. I couldn't tell if I'd pissed him off with the quip or wounded him. Maybe both.

"Get the fuck off me," I said.

Don's eyes narrowed. I could see the tiny wheels turning inside the pea where smarter men have brains. "No."

"I'm not playing around with you, dickhead," I said. "You're not gonna shove me into a locker anymore; or shove your dirty jockstrap in my mouth."

"You fucking loved that."

"I'm gonna love ripping your head off and making you eat your own asshole if you don't get off me."

"You like me on top of you," Don said in a metered voice. And then he smiled. "Oh, fuck yeah—you're already boned up and dripping like a leaky faucet, dude."

Don unshackled one of my wrists and reached between my legs, the surge of itchy pins and needles so powerful that, at first, I didn't realize I'd been released.

"You fucking *love* it," Don said.

I slid my hand onto the bulge at the front of his crotch and discovered the idiot from upstairs loved it, too.

Our eyes met, held.

Don flashed a shit-eating grin. "You want my dick."

"And you want to be a guest on 'Springer.'"

My enemy's smile waned. "You got a fucking mouth on you. How about I shut it? Stuff my hairy bone down your throat to quit all your bitching?"

"You can try," I challenged.

We struggled again, but only to undo buttons and zippers. Clothes dropped along with inhibitions. Don's balls, as meaty and hairy as I'd imagined while rubbing out my morning load that first morning on Height Street, tea-bagged my nose.

"Lick the sweat off my nuts, fucker," he commanded.

And just like that, we assumed those old roles, tough guy and tool mastering the conquered and cock-lover. I drew in a deep whiff off his sac, grew higher on the stink.

"Fuck," I sighed, my breath tickling his balls a step ahead of my fingers. Then I sucked them, Don's left nut first, his right second. Somehow, I managed to get both of his big stones in my mouth at the same time, something the fuck-tard clearly appreciated.

"Oh hell, yeah," he grunted, pulling up while I gulped down.

The tug of war waged on his balls further loosened them. I rubbed Don's nuts over my nose, licked at the funky patch of skin between his bag and asshole, stole a few licks on his pucker before the thrill of dominating me drove him to make good on the threat of filling my mouth with his meat.

"Do it," Don commanded. He smacked me across the face, driving home the level of danger that had jumped out of the past and into our present.

The Mastered sucked the Master's cock between his lips. Humming, I absorbed the details as, inch by inch, Don's dick disappeared down my throat: long and lean, like the rest of him, with plenty of veins, including a thick blue one running along the underside ridge, his junk covered in musk-stinking fur.

"Fucking cocksucker," he growled.

Sucking Don's dick to the balls, I showed him that I was also the *best*.

The stagger into my bedroom passed in the same violent blur as the kitchen's playground-style scrum.

"I don't do this shit," Don said, giving me a two-handed shove.

"You fucking liar. I bet you crave dick more than I do."

Don pushed me onto my bed. "Fuck you."

"Prove it," I reached into the top drawer of my nightstand, pulled out a foil packet and tossed it at him.

Don caught the condom with an underhand grab. "I'm not a homo, dude," he said, while rolling the skin down his dick faster than I'd ever seen a sock go on a cock.

Don spat on his dick for lube, lined his head up with my opening and pushed. My cock, pinned beneath his taut midriff, nearly burst under the pressure above and beneath as he entered me.

"Fucking animal," I huffed. "*Loser.*"

"Come-drunk whore," Don fired back.

"Stink-footed ape."

"I own your cunt."

"You should get so lucky, you stupid low-rent penis with feet."

In mid fuck-thrust, Don cracked up. I followed suit, set one hand on his chest, tracing circles in the sweaty chestnut hair, and pumped my dick with the other.

"I think it's gonna be fun having you so close to nark on."

"You shouldn't do that too often if you're not used to it," I grunted through clenched teeth.

"Do what? Nark your ass?" He slapped my thigh, hard.

I winced. "No, bonehead. *Think.*"

A few hours later, sucking on Don's toes, I conceded that yes, fun times in this town that I suddenly loathed less were a definite possibility.

HATFIELD AND MCCOY

Jay Starre

Just across the Kentucky state line in West Virginia, Bobby Hatfield ran a small filling station and garage. At only twenty-three, he was considered young to have his own business, but his rich Uncle Clay had been generous in providing the loan for starting up and Bobby had surprised everyone by working diligently night and day.

Only a few miles back in Kentucky on the other side of the Tug Fork, the stream that marked the border between the two states, Sean McCoy worked at his daddy's drugstore as part-time manager. He spent his free time taking college courses through the Internet and was determined to get an engineering degree—eventually. He had no intention of spending his whole life working for his daddy.

Of course, every young man has to escape his responsibilities now and then. Sean McCoy had been feeling fidgety all that sweltering, late-July day long and finally decided he'd had just about enough of Aunt Bertha, Cousin Nancy Jean, and his mom gossiping in the living room about all their sinner neighbors; and his daddy and Uncle Mitchell on the front porch gossiping about their other dang fool neighbors who couldn't hold their liquor or pay their bills. He'd gone to church that morning—*all* morning—and suffered through Sunday dinner with the relatives. Now, he just had to get away. He quietly snuck out the back door and slipped into the front seat of his pickup. He started it up and immediately gunned the engine to tear out of the driveway before his daddy could question him.

He didn't escape without notice. Mr. McCoy rose from his wooden chair on the porch and hollered out to him, "Where ya off to, Sean? Don't you be draggin' in late, you hear? You got to open up the store at seven A.M. in the mornin'!"

Sean didn't bother shouting back, but did stick his arm out the truck window and wave as a tacit acknowledgment of the order. He grinned as he briefly fantasized raising his middle finger and waving that at his daddy; but he wouldn't dare do that.

Half an hour later, he was across the Tug Fork and pulling into a little gas station in West Virginia. At almost eight in the evening on a Sunday, he was lucky to find anything open.

"Fill it up, please, sir."

"Sure thing, *sir!* Where y'headed? Come over the state line for some sight-seein'?"

The lanky, redheaded attendant looked just about Sean's own age, and he was pretty sure the guy was poking fun at him. Sean's truck had Kentucky plates, but it was only a few miles back. And the "sir" he'd used was definitely offered with some grinning sass.

Still, it was a nice enough grin, crooked and cute. The redhead was pretty dang handsome: green eyes, freckles across a strong nose and broad cheeks, dimpled chin. The guy was either attempting to grow a beard or he just hadn't bothered shaving for the past week. He had a little gold earring in his left ear and a colorful tattoo splashed across one muscular bicep and bare shoulder: a bare-breasted mermaid was breathing fire and below the fish tail, the words CONFEDERACY FOREVER were emblazoned in bold blue.

The fellow's tank top and cutoff jeans were spotted with oil and grease stains. Sean wondered if his boss would have approved of his outfit, or his attitude. His own daddy would never have tolerated either one.

"So, sir," redhead asked, "What brings you all the way over to West Virginia on a Sunday evenin'? A bit of cattin' around?" His smirk was matched by a mischievous twinkle in his eyes. Sean suddenly realized he'd been caught in the act of checking out the attendant in the side-view mirror. He leaned out the window and turned around to look directly at the attendant as he filled the tank behind him.

"It's dang hot out tonight. I'm lookin' for a spot to swim and cool off. I was thinkin' of Crook Bend."

"Naw, that place is gonna be crowded with damn fools drinkin' and fightin' and such tonight. I'll show ya a right nice spot. Just hang on while I close up."

Surprised and uncertain, Sean called out to the attendant's back as he jogged over to the station door and slammed it shut, then locked it. "Won't your boss be mad at ya for leavin'?"

The attendant turned and flashed that grin of his. "I *am* the damn boss!" Then he jogged back to the truck, climbed into the passenger seat and settled beside him. It had all happened so fast, Sean couldn't do much but laugh and go along.

"Follow that dirt road. It's not more'n five minutes from here. My secret spot. No one is gonna catch us skinny-dippin'."

Skinny-dipping? As the pickup began to bounce over the rutted track, Sean glanced over at his new buddy and wondered just how crazy this dude actually was. Swimming naked in a mountain pond wasn't exactly scandalous—locals had been doing it for generations—but it sure wasn't something his daddy would approve of.

Another glance at that bold tattoo on the redhead's muscular shoulder was enough to stir his already rising cock into a full-blown boner. He felt his face flush as his hands trembled on the steering wheel. How was he going to hide a hard-on if they were going skinny-dipping?

The bumpy ride down the wooded track was all too brief as Sean unsuccessfully willed his stiff cock to subside. The redheaded gas-station attendant was no help in that regard. He chattered on about heaven-only-knew-what in that deep, sexy voice of his, smirking and winking. Then to make it all impossibly worse, he dropped one hand to clap it over Sean's bare knee and squeeze.

The road ended in a little turnaround with the dense oak crowding in on three sides and the stream burbling by on the fourth.

"Here we are! Let's get nekked!" Redhead leaped out of the truck before they'd completely come to a jerking halt.

A rocky shore jutted out over a pool. It was definitely private, and it did look refreshing. Sean followed the redhead out of the truck and picked his way to the rocks. Red was already stripping off his tank top and cutoffs and dang! He wore no dang underwear! Now that was something Sean's daddy would never approve of. The redhead faced away from him and Sean got a good look at the guy's body: broad shoulders and muscular arms, a narrow waist and jutting butt. He was smooth all over and tanned, except for his blinding-white ass. Sean's stiff cock throbbed at the view.

True, Sean's body was nothing to be ashamed of. He'd been

working out with weights since he was barely a teen with his cousins in their garage. He wasn't as tall as Red, but his body was thicker with muscle, and dusted with hair as black as the wavy hair on his head—inherited from his handsome daddy, along with his big brown eyes.

The redhead let out a whoop as he leaped off the rocks and into the water. While Red was under the water and couldn't see Sean's boner, he seized the opportunity to kick off his sneakers, tear off his T-shirt and hop out of his shorts and skivvies.

Just as the other boy came up for air, Sean jumped in. He wasn't sure, but he feared those smoky green eyes had gotten a brief look at his bouncing hard-on before it disappeared beneath the water.

Sean felt the cool water envelop him and prayed that his boner would subside. But as he too came up for air and began to tread water, he was embarrassed to realize he'd had no such luck. Especially since he faced his new pal, and he was close enough to touch.

"Well, here we are," the guy said, a little breathless from treading water. "So, you gonna tell me your name, now that we're practically in each other's arms?"

"I'm Sean McCoy."

"Well ain't that a hoot. I'm a Hatfield. Bobby Hatfield. A damn McCoy and a damn Hatfield nekked together." Even though the feud between the two mountain clans was more than a hundred years in the past, smoldering resentments still existed. For many of the locals, the civil war had never ended; and neither had the infamous feud between the Hatfields and the McCoys. Many were the times Sean had heard his daddy and grandaddy say the Hatfields were "no good," and "downright filthy."

"Sweet!" Bobby said through a grin. "Just don't be telling your daddy, and I won't be tellin' mine!"

By that point, the two had paddled their way a few feet closer to shore where the bottom of the stream was suddenly underfoot. Bobby rose to stand in front of Sean with his upper body exposed from just below the chest. Both of his perky pinkish nipples were pierced, a little gold ring shining from each. Sean sucked in a breath: he'd never, ever seen the like. This Bobby Hatfield was definitely something else!

Beneath the water, a hand grazed Sean's thigh. His body twitched and he gasped out loud. He flushed easily and he was sure he was beet red as he looked up into the bold green eyes and sputtered out a reply.

"The last thing I'll be doin' is telling my daddy about this."

Bobby's trademark smirk grew broader as that hand beneath the water suddenly found his bobbing cock, and grabbed hold.

"So, you won't be tellin' daddy about this?" He squeezed Sean's hard-on and began stroking it. "How about this?" Bobby leaned down and kissed Sean, opening Sean's lips with his own and probing Sean's mouth with his tongue. Sean's skin turned to gooseflesh as he gave himself up to Bobby's hand and mouth. Bobby's other hand found his beneath the water and pulled it to his crotch. Sean found Bobby's pipe-thick tool and immediately began to pump it.

The Hatfield continued his sloppy kisses while he pushed his new McCoy pal backward and into shallower water. With their hands on each other's rearing pricks, and tongues now dueling, Sean knew he was all in, whatever came next. The Hatfield boy obviously figured as much. He broke their kiss and fell to his knees in the water.

"Time for me to suck some McCoy cock! You don't mind waitin' yer turn, do ya?"

With a wicked grin, he dove for Sean's twitching boner. Just as eagerly and sloppily as he'd kissed Sean's mouth, Bobby engulfed the thick tube with his lips and began to swab the mushroom head with his tongue. Sean groaned and shoved upward into the wet mouth as he leaned back and anchored his hands on the shallow bed of the pond. It was smooth rock like the shelf above and he squatted down on it and pumped his hips upward toward Bobby's hungry mouth.

The redhead worked on Sean's quivering cock, sexy green eyes staring up at Sean with a brazen, daring look. Suddenly, still slurping cock, Bobby grabbed Sean's knees and tipped him over backward. In a split second, Sean was on his back with his feet in the air. The water was shallow enough for him to lie back with only his torso submerged, his face and head above water. His eyes widened in amazement as he watched Bobby let his lips slide up and off his boner, then kiss his way down the underside of Sean's dick, give one quick lick to his tightly-bunched ball sac, and finally plant one of his wet, sloppy kisses right-smack-dab on the dark-haired McCoy's smooth, snug asshole.

That was definitely a first for Sean. He thrashed like a beached fish in the shallow water, bare feet waving in the air, his heart pounding in his chest as he gasped for breath. Lips that had just left his cock now sucked his butthole. The fat, insistent tongue that had recently probed his mouth and then licked his knob, now poked at his quivering asslips.

"Oh my lord!" he gasped. "What are you doing?"

Bobby's flushed face surfaced briefly. "Eatin' yer butthole. What did ya think? Ahma sit on your cock next! Tell me to stop if ya can't take it."

"No!" Sean stammered, "I mean fuck yeah! Eat my hole!" The thrill of the hot Hatfield boy tongue-fucking his hole—an act so nasty he'd hardly imagined people did such things—was nearly matched by the thrill of hearing Bobby talk so nasty, and then talking nasty right back. If Daddy heard that kind of language coming out of his mouth, let alone saw what Bobby Hatfield was doing with *his* mouth—he'd have a heart attack!

At the moment, Sean felt close to having a heart attack of his own. His entire body jerked and splashed around as Bobby pulled Sean's asslips apart with his fingers and stabbed at the gaping entrance with his tongue, tickled around the rim of it with rapid strokes, then jammed that hot tongue right into Sean's gut.

"Oh my lord, oh my lord," Sean repeated over and over, like a sinner at a revival meeting. He felt like he was melting into that greedy mouth and could have wallowed in the ass-eating for hours, but Bobby had already stopped and risen to his feet.

"Eatin' that tight ass of yours makes my own hole hungry for some action. You got a real fat dick and I intend on gettin' it up my butt, right now! I got some lube in my shorts. I'll be right back."

He was true to his word. Sean barely had time to catch his breath before the slim Hatfield was splashing his way back to the sprawled McCoy. He stepped up to place his feet on either side of Sean's chest and then bent over, facing the McCoy's feet and filling Sean's eyes with the view of his beautiful round ass.

"You got to lube up my asshole before I can sit on your dick. Use a couple of your fingers. I need it stretched out pretty good so I can take that fat pole of yours." Bobby's ass hung over Sean's face, pale and round as the moon, and about as inviting as anything he'd ever seen.

Sean's lube-slick hand shook like mad as he reached up and aimed two glistening fingers at the puckered slot in the center of Bobby's deep asscrack. He felt that hole twitch around his fingertips as he poked at it, then open outward as he pushed in, testing the sphincter.

"Yeah," Bobby said in a husky whisper. Shove 'em in there. Show no mercy. Otherwise I'll be hollerin' and bitchin' when I try to get that fat cock of yours in me."

Sean was so nervous and excited he was seized with a fit of giggling. But as his fingers slid past the snug rim and into the warm, moist pit beyond, the giggles turned to groans. His cock lurched and dribbled at his crotch as he imagined how those quivering anal walls were going to feel wrapping around it. He probed deeper and was amazed at how Bobby's hole swallowed him up.

"That's fine, McCoy," Bobby finally said. "Real fine. Now I got to get some big old dick up my butt!"

He rose off Sean's fingers and twisted around. His green eyes locked on to Sean's golden-brown ones, he squatted over the McCoy's lap, grabbed hold of Sean's cock, positioned the leaking head between his spread asscheeks and sat.

Hole met knob, then immediately began to gulp it up. The look on Bobby's face was absolutely amazing. His pert nose crinkled up, his beautiful green eyes squinted half-shut and his round mouth pursed. He snorted, then grunted like a gored pig as his butt-lips slowly and steadily stretched open for the plump cockhead. Sean couldn't help himself and he jerked upward, which only forced more cock up the juicy vise of Bobby's butt. Bobby laughed out loud and squatted down harder, driving even more hole down over Sean's cock.

"Tug on my nipples," Bobby commanded. "Go 'head, grab the rings and pull on 'em."

Totally in Bobby's thrall, Sean did what he was told: he reached up and seized the dangling gold rings attached to each small pink-brown nub. He'd intended to tug them lightly, but Bobby was squirming wildly over the cock burrowing up his ass, and his chest heaved just as wildly. Sean ended up yanking on the tender nipples, which made the redhead laugh louder and thrash around more violently.

Before he knew it, Bobby was riding his cock all the way to the balls, while thrusting his chest into Sean's tugging fingers. It was absolutely insane. Yet Bobby was hardly content to leave it at that. He suddenly reared up, the cock up his butt squirting out with a splash of lube, then fell forward to kneel over Sean's face and jam his throbbing-hard cock between his gasping lips.

"Suck me for a minute before I take another ride on that dick!"

Sean gurgled around the tapered head of Bobby's cock as the redhead pumped it in and out of his mouth, face-fucking Sean like a madman. Bobby's stiff meat was thicker toward the base, and Sean's lips stretched and slobbered as more and more cock drilled into his mouth.

He released his hold on Bobby's nipple rings and reached around to grab his butt. The heaving cheeks were slick with lube, sweat and pond water; satin-smooth skin over hard, clenched muscle. Sean's hands slid into the deep divide between Bobby's asscheeks. As cock pumped his mouth, his fingers found Bobby's puckered hole, and (almost with a mind of their own) jabbed up into it.

"Hell yeah!" Bobby rasped, his hips still fucking Sean's mouth. "Finger-fuck my hole. Feel how much your big damn dick stretched it out!"

It was true. The hole was not nearly as tight as it had been. Two of his fingers slipped beyond the sphincter and into the steamy innards. He crammed them deep and twisted, pushing Bobby's cock deeper into his mouth.

True to form, the Hatfield abruptly yanked his cock out of Sean's mouth and moved back to sit on his cock again. Grunting and squirming, he squatted down over Sean's lap to engulf his boner in steamy gut. He bounced up and down, water splashing around them as it suddenly began to grow darker. The sun was setting and it was nearing nightfall.

Bobby Hatfield was undeterred. He alternated between fucking Sean's cock with his ass, and fucking Sean's face with his cock; first one, then the other. The sprawled McCoy hovered on the brink of orgasm for what seemed like half an hour before he finally gave in to it.

"Oh my lord! I'm shootin', Bobby Hatfield! I'm shootin' right up yer asshole!"

"Hell yeah, Sean McCoy! Blow yer load in me! Here's mine! Here's my fuckin' load, McCoy!"

As he slammed his lush ass up and down over Sean's spurting cock and milked it dry, his own stiff rod shot out a geyser of gooey jizz. It flew so far it landed on Sean's gasping mouth. His head spinning, he snorted in the stink of it, and without a second thought, licked it off his lips.

Bobby let him up after that, but wasn't through with him. By moonlight, he led Sean deeper into the pond, and used his hands to wash all that lube and cum off him. When Bobby's probing hands moved into his big solid butt and began exploring, Sean knew what would be coming next.

"You fixin' to fuck my ass? May as well get myself butt-fucked, seeing as how my daddy would already be dang pissed at me for fucking your butt. And all the rest."

Bobby laughed before planting his lips on Sean's, silencing them both. This time the kiss was a little more languid, but the fingers in his crack weren't so polite. Underwater, one of them wormed up into him and twisted. He knew he was in for some more wild shenanigans. His family was right: the Hatfields were no good and downright filthy.

And that was just fine by this McCoy.

THE ONE IN THE MIDDLE

Dominic Santi

I love being fucked while I'm kissing a man who's being fucked. My boyfriend, Peter, shares the same proclivity. We also like variety in our shared lovers. For both Peter and me, an evening of ménages with friends is the hottest sex in the world.

Unfortunately, we both like to be the one in the middle. After a good deal of very satisfying experimentation, we decided the best way to get what we wanted, every time, was to share our favorite position. So now, when other men join us in our queen-size bed—a frequent occurrence in our sex-soaked boudoir—Peter and I, lip-locked like copulating snakes, become "the one in the middle" together.

Fuck, it gets me off. Peter's favorite position for the rest of his body is lying on his back with his head in the middle of the bed, his hips on the edge. His sun-bleached hair falls softly on the pristine white sheets, his gray eyes sparkling as he grins. Tonight he shoves a pillow under his ass and lifts his legs, tipping back so his half-hard dick lies leaking on the line of dark-blond hair leading down from his belly button to the tiny thatch of his pubes. Just looking at him makes my dick drool.

His shoulders wriggle against the sheets, his muscles flexing. The band of Celtic knots around his right biceps dances as he grips his knees. He pulls his tanned, lightly furred thighs up and out, spreading them wide over the ocean of one-thousand-count Egyptian cotton beneath him. We're both such sensation sluts. Just seeing him moving on the bed is so fucking hot.

I kneel on the opposite side of the mattress and bend over, my ass in the air, my weight on my elbows. My arms rest beside his left shoulder, close enough that I can feel the heat radiating off his skin. Close enough for me to appreciate the contrast of my darker skin beside his. I lean over to kiss him, long and slow and wet.

"Hey, sweetie," he whispers as we both come up for air. I laugh and kiss him again, moaning in pleasure as we both wriggle against the soft cotton sheets. Our sheets put a huge dent in our budget. After every night of ménages, we're buried in laundry. But it's so fucking worth it.

For a moment, I ignore the voices around us, but I can't help smiling. Kyle has stepped up between Peter's legs. My honey hasn't seen him yet: short, stout, muscular Kyle with the buzz-cut black hair and ripped abs and the nipple rings shining in the dark fur covering his chest. His dick isn't particularly long, but it's the thickest slab of man-meat I've ever seen. There's no way in hell I'd let him up my ass. Peter knows this. He knows my little pink sphincter puckers shut when I think of it.

Peter always lets him in. What I love best is sucking my sweetie's tongue while he's first being penetrated. He goes all soft and sensitive. His entire body is so relaxed and loving and, well, *receptive*. It makes my own ass hungry to be filled. Desperately hungry.

With Kyle's first touch, Peter moans in anticipation. The sounds Peter makes tell me what Kyle is doing: a long, slow rim job. Lots of lube and stretching. Then more lube—a lot more. Peter and I kiss and suck, moving just enough to keep my arms from going numb, loving each other's mouths, playing with our dicks, breathing as one man as we offer our holes to the men who will take pleasure from them.

I shudder in bliss as fingers stroke me, tongues rim, and cocks take turns sliding in and riding me hard. I kiss Peter, sharing my pleasure with him. I've been fucked by four guys by the time Kyle starts inching up Peter's ass. I haven't come yet, but my hole is deliciously loose. My joy-spot hums as my dick goes hard and soft and hard again while I kiss and tongue my honey's mouth. Peter pants and moans. He whispers filthy, pleading fuck words, telling me how his shaft is leaking onto his belly as Kyle works him open.

"It burns!" he pants against my lips. "Unh, unh, UNH!" His breath is warm and frantic. He smells of Bacardi and Coke and the Thai food we had for dinner. He tips his head back, opening his mouth wide, giving me his tongue to suck. When I open my eyes, I can see Kyle's wrists, showing just beneath the rounded edges of Peter's balls. Kyle's arms are moving slowly and firmly, rocking side to side, ruthlessly stretching my sweetie's asshole open. Kyle meets my eyes, grinning wickedly. He holds his arms wide apart, pulling until the cords pop in his forearms.

"Open," he growls. Peter keens into my lips.

Precum sluices through my dick. Ricco is fucking me. I recognize the delectable curve of his long, slender dick. He shafts me slowly, sliding exquisitely through my well-used asslips. He doesn't mind being fourth. He likes a leisurely fuck in an accommodating hole. Mine is exceptionally accommodating. His balls bounce softly against mine. I suck Peter's tongue, my lips tightening as I draw him deep. My asshole twitches in a futile attempt to clench Ricco's shaft. He laughs and fucks me harder.

"Don't even think about it, dude." His balls slap against mine. "Your hole's so loose I could drive a fucking truck through it!" I groan as he grinds deep. "Or my big ol' dick!"

Peter shivers and opens his mouth wider, giving me more of his tongue as he groans against me. I close my eyes, listening to the *slap, slap, slap* of Ricco's balls against my sac, enjoying how my lover enjoys hearing the sound of me being fucked.

Peter's next moan is softer, the shiver deeper. Kyle has taken one glistening hand from Peter's ass to grab the lube. He holds the bottle over Peter's ass and squeezes out another long, clear stream. Peter shudders. He has told me so often how he loves the cold shock of lube inside him, just before he's pierced by a big hot cock. I take his shudder in my mouth, kissing him, kissing and kissing and kissing while Ricco's cock thrusts in my hole, until finally I have to come up for air.

Kyle's grin splits his face. While I was distracted by Peter's tongue, Kyle has covered himself with a thickly ribbed condom. My sweetie is all about sensation. Kyle pours lube on his fat monster. I smile against Peter's lips, kissing him again, my lips curving so much I almost break the connection between us.

Peter's moans are getting louder. Kyle has one hand on Peter's hip, the other guiding his sledgehammer dick in. Ricco is fucking me more slowly now, but his cock is twitching. He's breathing hard. He is close to coming, but he's trying not to bounce me around too much while Kyle is sliding in. Ricco knows Peter needs me sucking his tongue to keep him relaxed enough to take that huge, meaty slab.

Despite our deep tongue-kissing, Peter's body is tightening. Wordless cries vibrate against my lips. Kyle is pressing through my honey's gate. My body stiffens, too, my ass trying to squeeze Ricco's cock.

"Easy, dude," Ricco murmurs, stroking my back. He pauses with just the tip inside me, holding me open, making me wait to be fucked again as I force myself to relax my body, relax my mouth. With my lips soft and dripping spit, I shove my tongue in Peter's mouth, breathing with him, helping him keep his mouth open, helping him stay open, keep his asshole open as Kyle relentlessly presses in.

My eyes are open wider than my hole. I can see both of Kyle's hands, one on Peter's hip, one holding his cock steady as he leans forward, spearing Peter's ass. Peter's breath is frantic, his cries almost sobs.

"Jerk your cock," Kyle growls.

I close my eyes, twist my body so I can reach my cock, ignoring even the heavenly feel of Ricco sliding back through my asshole as I concentrate on the feel of Peter's tongue on mine, the feel of my hand on my cock as our tongues lash deeper, harder, stronger.

Peter's shoulder tenses against me, his hand moving in rhythm with mine. He strains, bearing down. Now he is sucking my tongue, drawing me in. He stiffens, then he is wailing into my mouth, vibration electrifying my tongue as he arches against me. Kyle's fat cock is sliding through my lover's hole. Peter cries like a wounded bird, wordless "eee's" piercing my ears as he trembles uncontrollably against me.

"Yeah, baby! Let me in!" Kyle's growl is deep and unyielding. He knows how much my lover needs the reassurance that Kyle is *not* going to stop—no matter how much Peter yells and shakes. No matter what. My sweetie's ass is going to be fucked and fucked well. His ass is going to be taken by a man who will not hear the word *no*. A man who has negotiated with him, in advance, that unless *I* say to stop, that man is going to fuck my honey's quivering, clenching hole until it milks the cum through the cocktube fucking him, until my lover howls as his own dick shoots.

Peter shrieks. I come on the sheets, my dick spurting as I frantically suck my lover's tongue. Ricco is laughing, pounding me hard and fast now, fucking toward his own climax as I shake beneath him. My ass is twitching. Ricco knows I'm coming, but that fucker won't stop. He knows that as much as I love being fucked, his dick isn't what's making me come. I'm coming because I know Kyle's cock is finally spearing deep up my honey's ass. Kyle's stiff sausage is tunneling through my sweetie's hole, stretching it so wide and making it burn so bad, my lover's dick can't help drooling. Peter's hand grips the side of my head, yanking my hair until it feels like he's pulling it out by the roots.

I open my eyes to see streams of precum oozing onto my sweetie's belly. His other hand is on his dick, pulling the flushed red skin over his stiff, slick shaft. Kyle is fucking deeply and slowly now. Peter's mouth is finally relaxing. He peppers my lips with light, frantic kisses. His lips are all over the place, like he can't control where they're landing. In back of me, Ricco stiffens and moans, shaking as he slams in deep, emptying himself up my ass.

I shudder through his coming, shake more as he slowly pulls free. I love feeling the difference between the thrust of a hungry dick and the leisurely retreat of a spent one. He steps away, then someone else steps in back of me. I hear a condom wrapper tearing. Lube squirts. A different, tenor chuckle. Jaden. I relax against Peter's lips. Jaden's dick is average, but he has huge, heavy balls and he lasts forever. He lasts as long as Kyle does.

Maybe I'll get to come again when Peter does. I love it when we come together. And Kyle will make sure my sweetie comes so hard he howls.

Kyle has lifted Peter's ankles to his shoulders. Kyle has one hand on the bed, supporting his weight. The other is wrapped firmly around Peter's balls, rolling them, tugging the wrinkled pink sac as Peter moans and arches up. Peter's balls are deliciously sensitive. He opens his mouth farther, sucks tentatively on my tongue, trembling softly as I moan and press against him.

Jaden's thrusts are deep and rhythmic, each long, slow stroke drawing sensation through the entire length of my chute. He grabs my hips, tipping me forward as he slides in deep—and grinds, right into my joy-spot. I buck up, crying out into Peter's mouth as hot precum leaks through my cocktube. Precum mixed with the last drops from my first orgasm. Fuck, oh fuck, it feels good! Peter sucks my tongue hard, his voice rising as he shudders against me.

Jaden reaches between my legs. He grabs my balls. Tugging. Squeezing. Just the right amount to make them climb my throbbing dick. Peter is bucking against me. Our mouths are open like anacondas, sliding on our spit as our tongues move frantically over each other. An unexpected cry rises in my throat. Jaden's dick is punching my prostate. The cum is rising from my balls, my almost painfully squeezed balls.

Peter bows up against me, his whole body stiff as a lance. His wails move over my teeth. Lava-hot cum erupts through my dick. Then Peter is shaking and howling, bucking against me while I jerk against him, our dicks spurting in blinding, perfect orgasms as I yell until my throat hurts.

Afterward, Peter and I lie quietly against each other, kissing and tonguing, our deep, rhythmic breathing once again perfectly matched as Kyle and Jaden fuck us until *their* dicks are finally spent, too. It takes them a long time, but I don't care. Peter doesn't seem to mind either. The air is ripe with the smell of sweat and ass and lube. The sheets are wet beneath us, and the voices of our lovers echo in the background. My hole is raw and tender. Peter's quivers tell me his is, too. We grin tiredly against each other's lips, letting our wasted holes bring pleasure to the men who have brought us such exquisite pleasure as well. Once again, we are both exactly where we want to be—sandwiched together as one man.

The one in the middle, together.

ART APPRECIATION

Thomas Fuchs

As Bobby leaned back in the chaise longue, he thought how peaceful it was there, by the pool. Quiet. Up at the house, the guys were talking, talking, talking. Most of the talk was about art. Leo, their host, was a big art collector. The party that afternoon was to celebrate and admire his latest acquisition, a Hockney drawing of palms sheltering a swimming pool; a scene meant, as Richard had explained, to evoke a summer afternoon in Southern California. Bobby thought it was nice but, preferring the real thing, he'd slipped away from the party to bask in the sun.

He'd found a towel and some sunscreen in the pool house, stripped off his clothes—all of them, including his Calvin Kleins, no tan line, please—and stretched out on the chaise. As he went to work applying the cream, he thought that in a way, he was a work of art—his biceps, triceps, forearms so carefully shaped, his sculpted chest, smooth and powerful, the abs he'd worked so hard to achieve—a perfect six-pack. Then it was on to his dick, with its fine, solid thickness. Richard had joked how it should be registered as a dangerous weapon: "You could beat someone to death with that thing."

Bobby went from applying the sunscreen to stroking himself, and quickly got hard, that really great feeling, the head pushing out from the foreskin, the whole thing getting pink, then darker, that delightful deep sensation flowing along its length and a tingling in his ass. He worked himself and worked himself, the sun blazing down on him so that the distinction between himself, the sunshine and the world around him dissolved and he was filled with that power surging through him in those delicious, shivering moments before he bucked and twisted and the jism shot out, burst after burst, gobs spattering his chest, then sliding down as he lay back, collecting in a shimmering ivory pool in the hollow between his pecs. He dipped his fingers into it and spread it over his chest and abs, rubbing it into his skin, the rich cream, the finest sunscreen there was; then he lay back, basking in the after-bliss.

Total contentment never lasts for long and after a while his thoughts drifted back to the house and all the sophisticated talk, much of it from Richard. He smiled, wondering if Richard's artsy friends could imagine what it was like watching porn with him, Richard commenting on the models and the action as though it was some kind of art film. He wasn't sure if Richard was serious about this or just joking. Richard was a nice guy, really, all in all. Certainly generous. Fun travel. Good companion. Except that sometimes he went on a little too much, lecturing like he was giving one of his classes. Not bad looking and in pretty good shape for an old guy. Thank god he wasn't fat. Always respectful. Not too demanding. Pretty easy to please, in fact. Bobby certainly had plenty of freedom.

The sound of a bolt turning interrupted his thoughts.

Someone was coming into the pool area through the door from the alley. If Bobby, stark naked as he was, had been less self-confident, he might have been embarrassed and tried to cover himself, but he just sat and waited to see what would happen.

It was the pool man: a good-looking, dark-skinned Latino stud in a company polo shirt and cutoffs. Not tall, but not too short. Good face, high cheekbones. Jet-black hair, carefully spiked. Nice biceps, big chest. Great thighs, big and bursting with strength. Altogether, pretty hot. RAMON was stitched in yellow just above his shirt pocket.

Ramon, busy with his equipment and supplies, didn't see Bobby for a few moments. When he did look up and catch sight of him, he stopped dead, was silent for a beat, and then said, "Oh, sorry man," but he didn't look away from Bobby or his crotch.

"No problem," said Bobby. He took his time reaching down for his briefs, then stood up and faced Ramon directly as he pulled them on.

What was on the verge of happening next was interrupted by the click of footsteps on the flagstone path leading down from the house.

It was Richard. When he got to the pool, he clearly recognized that he was interrupting something, but he nodded politely to Ramon and said only, "Come on, Bobby. They're serving lunch."

The meal—a sit-down for twelve, served by a butler—was, in its own way, a work of art: two plates, one a fish-shaped pastry complete with tail and scales, filled with thin, alternating layers of smoked salmon and a truffle-laced pate; the other a fruit dish, leaf-shaped slices of mango arranged around concentric rings of shimmering green kiwi and a heart of strawberry, the whole thing forming a large, exotic flower.

When several of the guests pulled out their phones to take pictures of the meal, Richard said, "You can't capture this in images alone. This art is meant for more than just our visual sense." Lifting his fork, he added, "Let us fully appreciate it."

Bobby ate quickly and as the butler cleared his empty plates, he asked their host, Leo, if it would be all right for him to take a swim.

"Sure," said Leo. "That's what the pool is for. There are suits in the pool house if you want one." Richard, deep in conversation with the woman next to him, seemed barely to notice Bobby leaving.

As he started down from the house, Bobby was relieved to see that Ramon was still there, vacuuming garden debris from the pool. His shirt was off and his broad back and shoulders were golden in the sun. Bobby's dick began to stir. When Ramon saw him, he flashed a grin that made it abundantly clear that he had been hoping Bobby would return.

There wasn't any small talk between them. No talk at all, in fact. They went into the pool house, a small, somewhat dank concrete room, furnished with a few rattan chairs and pillows.

Still without speaking, both men stripped and stood inches apart, appraising each other, growing increasingly excited by what they saw. Both were magnificent: in shape, well defined and nicely hung. Bobby was shaved; Ramon sported a nest of glossy black hair. Both were semihard.

Like professional dancers improvising a routine, they stepped toward each other, held each other. Bobby's dick sprang hard against Ramon, and Ramon's pressed into Bobby's thigh.

For both, touching each other was like embracing a finely carved statue, only warm and pulsing with life. Bobby licked a spot on Ramon's neck that made the Latin boy shiver and moan.

Now it was Ramon's turn to give pleasure. He slid down and

began flicking the tip of his tongue on one of Bobby's nipples (a touch, a touch, a touch), a rapid fire of stimulation, each contact distinct, each making Bobby ache all over with pleasure.

Again without a word and acting as one, they grabbed the pillows off the chairs and threw them on the floor to use as a bed where they explored every slope and crevice of each other's bodies with their fingers, lips, tongues.

When Ramon got to Bobby's dick, Bobby swung around so they could sixty-nine and began licking and sucking as Ramon did the same to him, repeating what he had done to Bobby's tit, teasing the tip of his prick with a rapid-fire series of tongue touches that overwhelmed him so that he neglected Ramon's cock and had to control himself to resume rewarding his partner with sensations as intense as those racking him.

After some time of this, Bobby tasted precum. Ramon was about to shoot and Bobby wasn't sure how much longer he could restrain himself. He pulled away and held himself to head off the explosion. There was a brief pause, a moment when neither was sure what would happen next.

Then Bobby decided and led the way. He didn't usually like to get fucked, but he wanted it now: maybe it was Ramon's thick, powerful thighs. He rolled onto his back, his legs up, his desire all but palpable. Ramon, flashing that grin, was clearly all for it.

Bobby started to tell him that he had a rubber and lube in his pants, but Ramon reached over to his own pile of clothes and fished out the necessities. He turned out to have a fine technique, not trying to ram it in but taking his time, using his cock to tease Bobby's asshole, getting it to relax and open so that he could slide right in as Bobby closed around him.

With a rhythm that was slow, steady, sure, he pumped deeply into Bobby, making him gasp and groan with pleasure. And then came a transition, a sliding change of tempo, Ramon pumping faster and faster, making Bobby writhe in the sweet agony of a really good fuck.

Finally, Ramon rammed in as deeply as he could, and Bobby caught him, using his ass muscles to squeeze Ramon and hold him tight. The Latin guy bucked his hips as Bobby squeezed harder until Ramon gasped, "Oh, fuck, fuck, fuck!" Bobby relaxed his hole and Ramon slowly pulled out, then stripped off the rubber and grabbed his cock, giving it a few final jerks while Bobby jacked his own bloated dick and suddenly there was cum everywhere.

Completely sated, both men lay back and rested. It was Ramon who, a few minutes later, sat up abruptly. "Geez," he said, "it's late. I've got to git." He toweled off, pulled on his clothes, said, "Well, that was fun," and left.

Bobby looked at his watch. The afternoon was almost gone. Richard would be ready to leave.

In the car, going home, neither said anything until Richard broke the silence with, "You might not have noticed, but our host's Hockney is a fake."

"What?"

"His newest acquisition," said Richard, "the piece we all came to see. It's a copy."

"Are you sure?"

"I'd have to take it out from under the glass, but I'm ninety-nine-percent sure. It's a new method. The original is digitized, then the forger goes over it by hand. It's a lot of work but it makes for a very good copy."

"Did you tell him?" asked Bobby.

"No." said Richard. "Why should I spoil things for him? He takes such great pleasure in it."

"But he's been ripped off."

"When he insures it," said Richard, "the appraiser will catch it. And if he doesn't, well, then, officially it's just as valuable as the real thing. Think of it this way. Art isn't an object. It's what happens between the object and the person experiencing it. Whether it's a picture, sculpture, music, dance, literature, it's the transmission of feeling that makes it art." And then without a pause, he went on to ask, "And speaking of experiencing things, did you have a good time this afternoon?"

"I did," said Bobby.

"Excellent. You'll tell me all about it tonight?"

"Sure."

"All the details?" asked Richard.

"Of course," said Bobby. "Don't I always?"

COACH'S PUSSY

Dan Cavanagh

The coach came into his office from the locker room, tucking his cock and balls back into his jock. A trickle of leftover piss ran down the hair on his heavy thigh. He palmed it off and wiped it on his sweaty T-shirt, then took his shorts from over his shoulder and threw them at Ken.

"Wanna smell, fucker?" he said through a broad grin, then turned his back to the kid, pressed his hands against the wall and began to stretch the kinks out of his calves.

Ken had come in from practice and had just finished cleaning up the coach's office when the huge man lumbered in. He sat on a low stool, staring up the crack of the coach's ass; watching the calves ball up and release as the man worked them; watching the asscheeks tighten and dimple. His palms began to sweat as he rubbed them up and down the golden hairs on the insides of his thighs. He was a freshman and had barely gotten in on a work-grant as a "team manager." He'd been a champion swimmer in high school; he was now a physics major in the classroom, and a flunky in the Athletic Center who would do anything the coach told him.

"I finished the laundry."

"Those assholes," the coach moaned as that good stretching pain traveled up one calf, then the other. "They'd leave stuff in their lockers until mold grew." He turned to face Ken. "Shit work, huh? But I bet you really get off on all those sweaty jocks. Huh, Kenny? Am I right? I found three of them in your locker."

And he smiled that perfect smile.

Ken's face flushed and his lips parted slightly as he drank in the man. Coach Yastic was forty-eight; six-foot-one of hard muscle under hairy, deeply tanned skin. Huge biceps stressed the seams of his sleeves, sleeves so short the armpit hair poked out underneath. Ken could trace the pattern of thick hair visible under the shirt; there was a fold of cloth stretched between fat nipples. The man's legs were massive and covered in black wire everywhere except the backs of his calves, where the bulk of them had rubbed against his jeans for years. And his cock, only semierect, pushed the jock pouch out with such force that in profile Ken could see the balls trying to work their way free.

Normally combed straight back, Yastic's black hair, graying at the temples, fell into an unruly mop of curls when he worked out. Ken's father had called him a man's man. He was married, but he could seduce with a smile and had been warned repeatedly about fucking coeds. But he always had a favorite, a "boy-tool" he laughingly called the kid: some punk stud panting around his heavy rod.

He'd promise a kid a "better body" and schedule late training sessions. Yastic would show up in gym shorts slit up to his hip and an athletic T-shirt dingy with age. He'd stand directly over the kid's head during bench presses, counting low and slow, giving the boy a direct view up between his thighs into the wet, rank crotch. He'd smile, watching the kid squint his eyes shut, fighting it; then stand there once the set was over, letting the boy inhale him with every gasping breath.

Ken had seen the results. He remembered Pete, Yastic's last piece—a short, redheaded wrestler with a muscle-boy build under paper-thin white skin. He'd watched Pete in class one day, squirming at his desk in crotch-high cutoffs during an American History lecture, his ass grasping as if trying to eat the chair beneath him. What Ken hadn't seen was, that night, the kid had sucked Yastic from head to foot; and before the evening was over, Pete's asshole had inhaled the man's hand to the wrist. The next day, the kid had an orgasm in class. Audibly, not even touching his dick: apparently, Yastic had treated the kid to a large butt plug. Pete was expelled the same day.

Yastic slumped into the chair behind his desk and pushed the chair away. Leaning back, he put his feet up on the edge of the desk, facing Ken.

"Lock the door." Ken did as he was told. Yastic lit a cigarette, clicked the lighter shut as he exhaled. "Let's see."

Ken slipped his T-shirt over his head and, reaching down, worked off his gym shoes. He reached for his shorts.

"Leave it."

He began his routine. He flexed his biceps, imitating the poses he'd seen in the muscle magazines. Yastic chuckled. Turning sideways, he twisted his torso and worked his lats, putting one foot behind the other and rising up on his toes.

"Hold it." It was an awkward position. Ken trembled. "Hold it, Kenny-boy."

The routine was ridiculous. Yastic knew it; Ken knew it. He had a beautiful, smooth swimmer's body with big pink nipples and hard long muscles. But the "muscleman" poses were humiliating.

Yastic exhaled. "You're comin' along, baby."

"Thank you, sir."

"You make me proud. Are you happy for me?"

"Yes, sir."

"You like makin' me proud?"

"Yes, sir." He was beginning to sweat.

"How proud is that, baby?"

"Real proud, sir."

"Then come over here and show me how much."

He broke the pose and walked slowly over to Yastic. He stared at the man and waited for the next instruction. When nothing came for what may have been a minute or two, he timidly bent down and crawled between the man's legs that still rested on the desktop. He brought his head up, feeling the heat from those thighs, and stared eye-level at the jock pouch. Another pause. He could hear Yastic talk through a smile.

"This one never gets washed. You understand that, baby?"

"Yes, sir."

"There's a lot of man-spit on that jock. If you're really lucky, I'll let you wear it up your asshole for a day. You like that?"

Ken was breathing quickly.

"Yes, sir."

"Huh?"

"Yes, sir." he repeated, louder.

Yastic ran his hand into the pouch and pulled his rod up until the head was poking out over the top, glistening. He groped inside again and began to mash his balls hard. He groaned. Then he brought his hand out and held it out toward Ken.

"Kiss it."

Ken moved his lips against the hair on the back of the hand and inhaled. His cock was so hard it hurt. Yastic liked it that way: knowing his fuck-boy's cock was aching in confinement.

Ken began licking the funk, sucking. Yastic turned his hand palm up and Ken closed his eyes, taking each thick, calloused finger into his mouth and sucking on them one at a time.

"Nice. Real nice. Just like a pussy with a tongue, baby."

He felt the boy swallow each fingertip and stretch his tongue to reach for the hair on the back of the coach's hand. They locked eyes. Yastic tossed the cigarette on the floor, then reached down and took the boy's head in both hands. Pulling Ken's mouth into his crotch, he slowly brought his thighs together, tight, enclosing the head. He tilted his head back, crossing his legs at the ankles, squeezing tighter.

"Oh yeah...c'mon home, boy."

Ken's head disappeared completely in wet, straining thigh muscles and massive hands. His mouth and nose mashed hard into the jock material, drowning him in the smell of the man with every breath. His arms barely made it around the man's legs as his hands came up to stroke the thighs.

"You belong between this man's legs, Kenny baby. You know that? Shame you gotta waste your time in class when you oughta be studyin' how to make a man feel good. Daddy's gonna teach you."

Yastic released the boy's head, and he came up gasping for air. He scrunched down lower on the chair and rested his calves completely on the desktop. His ass was hanging over the edge of the chair now, his hole on a level with the blond boy's face.

"Get to work."

Ken's long, fine fingers barely spanned the massive ass globes as he reached up and pulled them apart. Yastic's bunghole opened wide immediately, as if it knew what was coming and reached out with a mind of its own to accommodate another fuck-boy. Groaning, Ken pressed his face into the hair, worked his head back and forth a few times to gain deeper purchase on the hole. Then he thrust his tongue in, all the way from the back of his throat.

Yastic locked his fingers behind his own head and leaned back with a sigh. His anal sphincter worked like a wet hand, opening wide, inviting the tongue and most of the pink boy-lips, and then clamping shut, pushing Ken's lips back out, but retaining the tongue. Ken would curl it hard up and down, working it as much as he could like a fingertip, ignoring the cramping this caused in the base of his mouth. He paused the action only long enough to gather saliva and force it into the hole.

"Deeper, baby," Yastic said to the ceiling.

Ken dropped his jaw and pushed harder.

The asslips tightened harder and yanked the tongue again. Yastic continued the routine until he could hear a squelching sound from the boy-man connection, the meeting of butthole and boy-mouth, saliva and ass-mucous.

"Now wiggle it."

With two fingers of each hand, Ken widened the bowel. Then, twisting his head from side to side as far as the ass-valley would allow, he wriggled his tongue frantically. His knee slipped as he rooted forward, like a pig in a trough.

The phone rang. It rang again. Ken finally heard it as his mind slowly rose to the surface.

He began to pull away when suddenly he felt his head pulled back hard by the hair. He had barely enough time to see the heavy hand come flying out of nowhere and smash him across the face. He stared wide-eyed into the shadow of Yastic's sweaty face as his cheek prickled with pain. The phone continued ringing.

"You don't stop unless I tell you, Kenny." The coach smiled. "You don't do anything unless I tell you. Isn't that right?" The phone rang.

"Yes, sir."

"That's five more strokes with the belt, now."

"Yes, sir."

"Don't worry, honey. You'll learn. Now show me how sorry you are."

Yastic brought his massive legs down on either side of the kneeling blond.

"Start at my feet."

Ken scooted backward and reached for the laces on the right running shoe, as Yastic picked up the phone.

He felt calf muscle spread across his hand like a heavy pillow as he lifted first one leg, then the other, to slip the shoes off. He slowly peeled the wet socks down the ankles and off the size-13 feet: gray-white socks pungent with man-smell.

He lowered his mouth. As he opened it, he could feel his asshole opening simultaneously. It reached out as his lips met the hair covering the top of Yastic's high-arched right foot. And then, as the mouth closed in suction, the asslips clamped shut. Suddenly aware of the emptiness in his bowel, he winced at the violent ache in his one hole, as he whimpered through the other.

He slavered over the foot, separating each long toe as he washed off the sweat between and under them. Using his tongue as a tool, he dug for dirt under the nails he'd clipped a week ago. Then he cleaned the tops of the feet, sucking man-taste from each pore until his cheeks ached with the vacuum he was creating. He'd been beaten for skipping the ankles once before, so he made sure to wrap his lips thoroughly around each, knowing he had to earn his way to the heavy muscles waiting above him. Gradually, he reached the back of the first calf and massaged the muscle, hair and wetness around his mouth like he was jacking a dick.

Yastic was chuckling into the phone.

"Sandpaper the stubble off the asshole. I did it every night before little Petey got himself expelled. Sandpaper him, belt his ass. What?"

Yastic sounded pissed.

"Give him fifty. Yeah, let him scream. After twenty-five, tie him down or he'll start bucking at you like a dog in heat. He can take it. After that you can fuck it for an hour. Hell no! That's what I was afraid of, but that ass is built for it. It couldn't get enough and the next night it was always white, tight and butter soft."

They were talking about Pete, the redheaded wrestler. Ken had walked in on them once. Pete had been lying on a massage table with his head dangling over the side, his mouth split wide as Yastic's cock snaked up the length of wet throat and back out again. Even from a distance Ken could see Pete's neck distort with the size of the cock-pipe every time it went in, the Adam's apple working in a disciplined rhythm, like a fist.

Yastic had had Pete's legs bent under his armpits, asshole at face level. Four of his huge fingers were buried up the ass and Ken could see his muscles straining with the effort as he pulled the muscled boy-hole open.

Suddenly, Yastic had caught sight of Ken standing in the doorway. Everything stopped.

Slowly, he raised his shaggy head. Then grinned a challenge.

He gradually began easing the cock out of the mouth-hole. Halfway out, Pete began whimpering. Yastic stopped, smiling at Ken. Then he withdrew some more. As the cockhead reached Pete's lips, the boy tried to slide toward it. Yastic held the cock-head there, barely contained in the boy's mouth.

Then, cruelly, he popped it out.

Pete wailed, like a baby who'd lost a bottle. His head whipped back and forth, and he began to pound the table with his fists. Yastic, even with his huge muscles, fought to hold him rock steady.

"Close the door, handsome," Yastic rumbled.

But Kenny backed out. He ran to the bathroom, reached a stall and bolted it just in time. Clinging to the top of the door with both hands, he threw his head back, eyes staring in surprise, as he came in his pants.

Yastic missed Pete. Kenny could hear it in the way the big man talked about him. "A fuckin' stud-pussy who knew his place. With two hungry fuck-holes." Yastic would grin. And then the grin would fade into a long silence, as if Ken weren't there.

When Kenny was jacking off in his dorm room, he usually came silently. But one night, he realized what he was, or what he wanted to be: Yastic's stud-pussy; a hot boy-body wrapped around two hungry fuck-holes that the big man used instead of his fist. Suddenly his back arched from the bed ("fuckin' stud-pussy") and he screamed for the first time in his young sex life. The sudden bulk and force of his semen was painful ("two hungry fuck-holes") as it shot into the springs of the bunk above him. When it was over, he lay there helpless in recovery as the cum dripped down on his body, his face.

His cheek was brushing against Yastic's jock strap now as he finally reached high inside one huge thigh.

The crotch smell was a drug. It could take his mind off his work and had gotten him into trouble before. He wasn't here to lose his mind on cock and muscle. He was here to service a man. Would Yastic expect him to rim his ass again? Had he pulled out too soon? He whimpered in fear. The big man didn't like to be asked questions. And Kenny's ass tucked forward as he anticipated the belting he'd receive if he made a mistake. He was already up to fifteen nightly, each mistake increasing the count by three to five strokes. The number never went down.

He felt Yastic's big hand, absently stroking his hair.

"Bring Petey over here. Be here in half an hour," he was

saying into the phone. He sounded sad. "I've got Kenny here up to twenty."

Tightening his fingers in the blond hair, he gently pulled the head back and stared into boy-face. The eyes were closed; the mouth hung slack and the face was coated with saliva.

"He's just pool pussy." Cradling the phone on his shoulder, he took one huge fist and began squeezing Ken's mouth like a piece of clay. He slapped it, then worked it again. Slap; squeeze. "I'd like to show him how a real athlete takes a fuck."

He chuckled at the response from the other end of the line and hung up.

He sat silently for a few minutes. The room was darkening as the sun went down. There were no lights on in the room.

Yastic stared, unseeing, into Kenny's face. He wrapped both huge hands around the back of the boy's neck. Pushing the jaw up with his thumbs, he tilted the head back and then slowly stroked the soft outside of the throat tube with his thumbs.

"Fuckin' pussy shit," Yastic muttered angrily.

Ken thought he was talking about him and froze in the half darkness, frightened, prepared for the worst. His head was immobilized as the huge thumbs gently jacked his throat.

"I work damn hard putting bulk on Petey, turn him into one hot little blue-eyed nut-cracker, bring out the best in him, and he craps out in the army."

He dropped his head with a sigh. Then raised it. He stared at Kenny as if seeing him for the first time.

"But look what I've got instead." Ken started to smile, but there was something in the man's tone that made him stop. "Team Manager." There was a long pause. Then...

"Shit."

Slowly, Yastic began to stand. Kenny found himself staring up the massive thighs, heavy muscles covered with hair. Their bulk shoved the jock forward, the pouch straining, stained and fraying at the seams. Yastic reached back absently and scratched the crack of his ass.

"Pool pussy. Fuckin' pool pussy."

He stood about a foot away from the blond. Then, slowly, he began to smile. He rubbed the bulk of his crotch with both hands.

"But we're gonna make this team manager a real locker room pussy boy." He grinned. Then, hooking both thumbs into the waistband, he began to lower the jock. His voice was low and steady.

"Keep you barefoot; speedos; cutoff T-shirt. My boys like to see swimmer's skin. Like to have it around." The huge cock eased out between the V formed by the wrists as the waistband descended. The cock nodded as if it were alive as the elastic slid down the contours of its length. The head pouted and a huge strand of pre-fuck drooled toward the floor. Once free, it stood rigid at a 45-degree angle.

"Give the team something to look forward to after the game."

The jock was half way down Yastic's thighs before the gonads swung free. He stepped out of it and flipped it on the desk. They swung gently between his spread thighs.

"They can earn your pussy on the field. I'll decide who gets it. Then you can wait in the shower and wash him down. Pecs, crotch. Sore, grimy feet. Make him real grateful. Afterward, he can press his hands against the wall while you give that ass a good, deep mouth rinse."

There was a pause. The head of Kenny's cock ached in confinement.

The room was silent. It was getting darker.

Suddenly Yastic's leg shot out. He hooked his big foot under the boy's crotch and yanked him violently toward the cock. Ken cried out as his knees skidded across the floor. Yastic slapped him hard. He grinned wider and reached for the boy's head with one hand. With the other he began to bend the cock down.

"When he's good and hot, he can bring your ass in here and fuck you on the table. You're gonna know just what he needs by then."

The bottom of Ken's jaw touched his Adam's apple as the cockhead entered his mouth. He pulled a muscle in his jaw, frantically trying to keep his teeth out of the way.

"If you're the kind of hot stud I'm training you to be, the fuck won't last too long."

Crushing the tongue to the floor of the mouth, the huge cock-pipe bored steadily down into the throat as the pink, wet tissues streamed slowly along its sides. Yastic chuckled.

"If you're lucky, though, it will."

Tears ran from Kenny's eyes. The cock reamed its way down like a long piston in slow motion. When Kenny's nose was mashed back by the man's hard stomach, Yastic stopped. He paused, savoring that special tightness he liked in a boy-throat. Then he began a slow, circular grinding motion, scouring the soft pink lips with the coarse, gray-black wire that lined his crotch. The huge stud and the blond head were one solid piece from the back of Yastic's ass down through to the top of the boy's chest.

"Not gonna take much time tonight, baby," Yastic moaned.

He began to fuck.

His pecs bulged as he slid the hole off his cock, then his ass dimpled as he drove the thing hard, full-length down the pit. Kenny moaned, stupid with need. Yastic withdrew.

He rammed.

Kenny's hands caressed the balls. Yastic withdrew. As the

mouth-fucking continued, Kenny could feel the spit dangle in strands from his mouth onto his wrists.

Yastic's head was thrown back. The face-fucking picked up speed. He began mumbling. Suddenly, calling the wrong name, he moaned, "C'mon, Petey! C'mon, Petey!" But his thrusts suddenly became wild as he used the face-hole like his own fist. He lowered his face, grabbed the head by the blond hair and yanked it toward him so hard that Kenny squealed. The boy marshaled his over-stretched muscles into a deep sucking rhythm, pleasuring the solid mass bursting the walls of his throat.

The corner of Yastic's mouth turned up and he snarled at the thing drooling and sucking at his feet. Finally he rolled his head back, his knees bent and he rammed upward, lifting the body off its knees as he forced the head down. His eyes rolled back in his head.

He shot.

Every muscle in his huge body stood out in relief. His brain was in his cock, slam-pumping huge gobs of cum into an open, eager stomach. There was one consciousness in the room: a virile man-stud and the thing attached to his prick. He watched cum begin to run from its nose.

When he was through with it, he yanked it off, threw it to the floor and fell back into his chair.

Five minutes later a lighter clicked on, illuminating a relaxed, sweaty face as the eyes looked at the end of the cigarette. He felt hands on his leg and a face resting against his calf. He pushed it aside. The lighter clicked shut. Then darkness.

Everybody's Doin' It

script: Dale Lazarov   art: Jason A. Quest

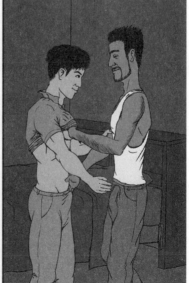

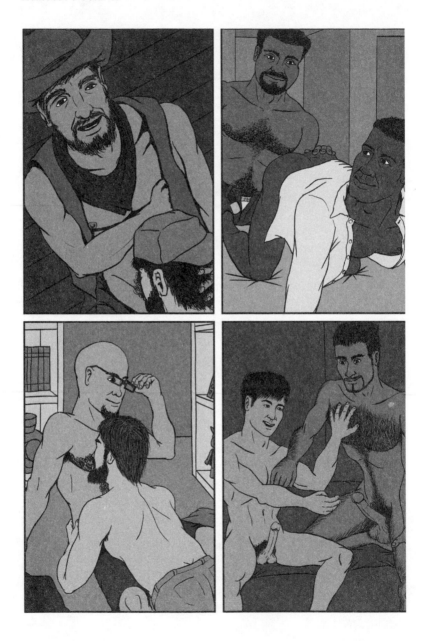

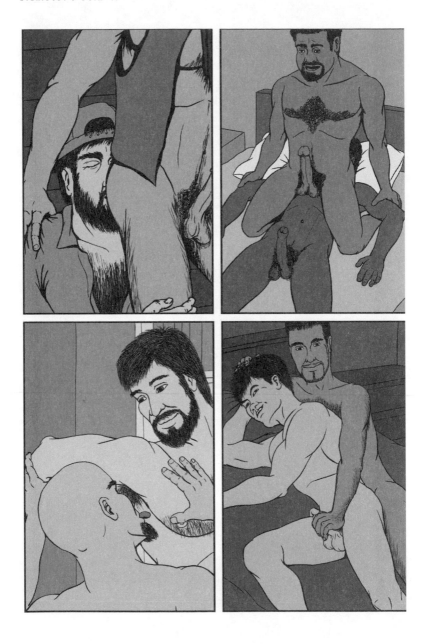

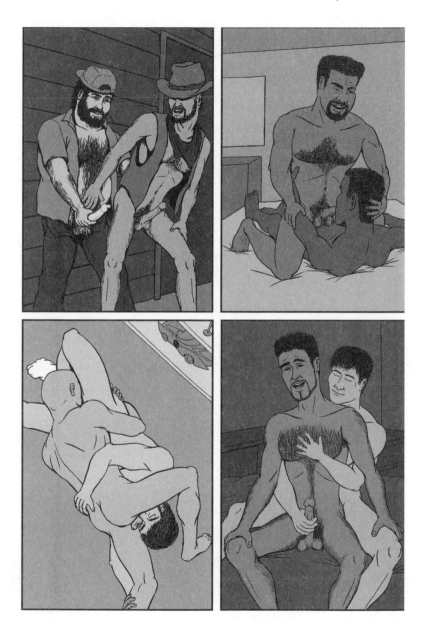

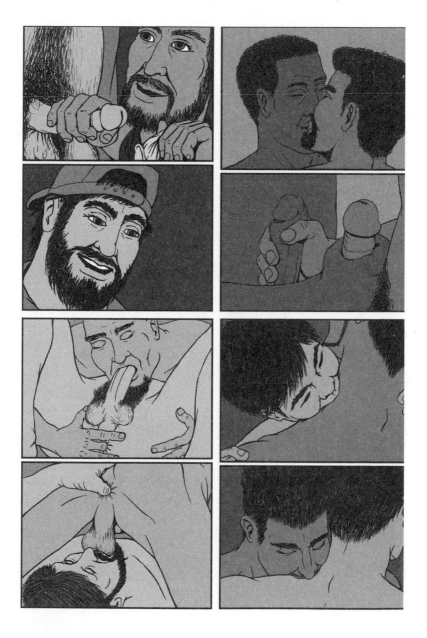

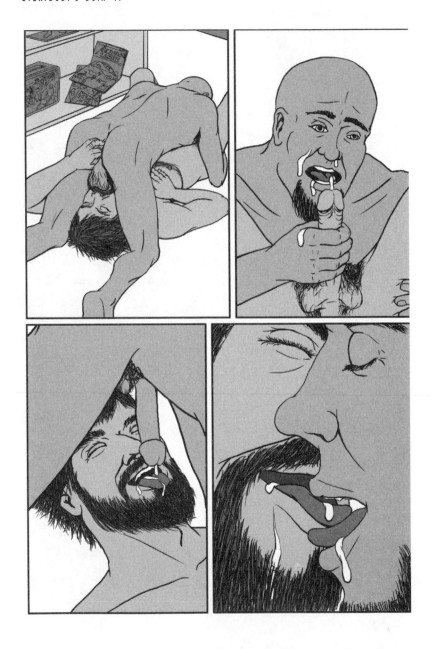

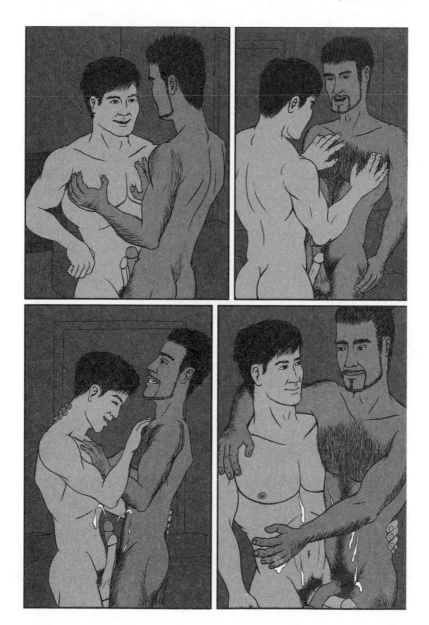

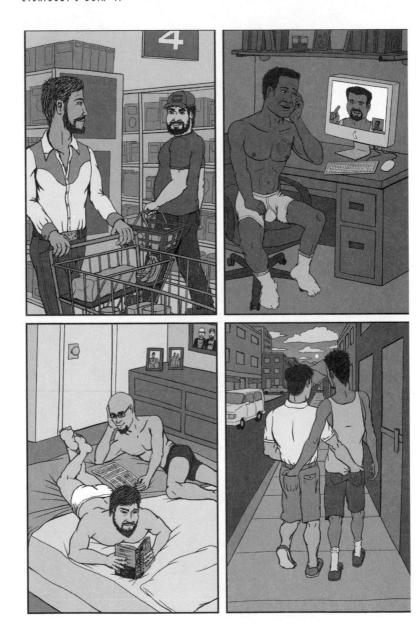

A WALK IN THE PARK

Max Vos

"That's the last box, Mr. Burke," the hunky mover said, setting a box on the floor.

"Thanks, Tim. You and your guys have been a great help." Burke could smell the sweaty man's scent wafting up, causing Burke's balls to draw up slightly.

"You're welcome, Mr. Burke." Tim shook Burke's hand one last time, leaving the apartment stacked with boxes, all in disarray.

Burke turned and sighed. "How 'bout a quick walk before we start unpacking, Sparky?" The Jack Russell terrier jumped and barked once, his stub of a tail wagging frantically. "Thought you might be up for that," Burke smiled, getting Sparky's leash out. "We'll try out that dog park. Whaddya say?"

Sparky pulled at the leash as they walked, stopping to sniff the shrubs here and there, obviously excited over exploring the new territory. Just as the two rounded the corner of the apartment building, Burke spotted a guy with an English bulldog puppy on a leash, also heading toward the dog park.

"Maybe you'll have a new playmate there, Spark." Burke spoke softly to his pet, who was tugging at his leash impatiently.

As Burke and Sparky opened the gate to the dog park, the English bulldog puppy rushed toward them, ready to play.

"Daisy, get back here," the owner of the puppy called, to no avail, rushing after his pup. Burke kept Sparky on his leash until he knew for sure that the two dogs would get along. When Daisy reached Sparky, they sniffed each other, both stubby tails wagging a mile a minute.

"Hey, sorry about that," Daisy's owner apologized. "She's still a puppy and doesn't mind very well yet."

"Hey, no problem," Burke said, staring into the topaz eyes of Daisy's owner. "I know how that is. I'm Burke; and this bundle of energy is Sparky." The terrier looked back as he heard his name, but immediately turned back to his new playmate, ignoring the human element.

"Hey, nice to meet you," Daisy's owner said as he stuck out a big fur-covered hand. "I'm Hank; Hank Staunton."

"Nice to meet you, too, Hank," Burke replied as he bent to undo Sparky's leash, letting the two dogs go off and play. "Actually, Burke is my last name, but it's what all my friends call me. My first name is Stanley, which I've never liked, so Burke works for me."

"Yeah, I understand. My real first name is Henry, which I don't care for, so Hank is fine by me."

Burke was all but knocked back by the smile Hank flashed at him. It had been over two years since his breakup with his former partner, and his hormones seemed to be in overdrive today. Since he was about to turn thirty-one in a few days, he figured it was time to get his shit together and move on, and leave the past behind.

The two men sat on the nearby bench and watched the two dogs play.

"This was the only apartment complex I could find that had a dog park," Burke said casually.

"Yeah, it's a nice complex. It's clean and they really keep it up," Hank said, chuckling at the two dogs playing tag. "You just move in?" Hank asked, turning his buttery-soft eyes toward Burke. "I haven't seen you around before."

"Yes," Burke's eyes locked onto Hank's. "Movers left a little while ago. I've got a lot to get done before next Monday when I start work."

"Welcome to the neighborhood," Hank said, as they watched Daisy and Sparky play tug-of-war with a stick. "By the way," he added, "I'm having a few friends over this Saturday night, if you wanna come by. If you're not busy that is."

"Um, sure," Burke stammered, slightly surprised by the invitation from someone he had just met.

"Hey, if you have other plans that's okay," Hank turned, sensing Burke's hesitation.

"No, it isn't that at all," Burke said looking at his shoe as he traced around a rock stuck in the ground. "It's...well Saturday is my birthday and I was kinda planning on staying in. You know, kicking back, relaxing."

Hank's mouth fell open. "What! Your birthday is Saturday?"

"Yeah," Burke grimaced slightly, not liking to attract attention to himself.

"Well I'll be fucked running with a jelly doughnut," Hank looked stunned, shaking his head.

"What is it?"

"Friday is *my* birthday," Hank laughed. "I'm turning the big three-oh!"

"Really?" Burke asked. "I'm going to be thirty-one."

"How cool is that?" Hank said excitedly. "We need to really throw a party, then. Feel free to invite some of your friends to come along!"

"Um, I just moved here, and I really don't know anyone."

"Well, you do now!" Hank said, bumping Burke's shoulder with his own.

"What was that thing you said about a jelly doughnut?" Burke asked, looking a bit confused.

"It's just an old sayin'," Hank chuckled. "I had an uncle that had a ton of 'em, and I guess I picked some of 'em up." Hank looked at the puzzled look on Burke's face and grinned. "Where you from, anyway?"

"Maryland. Gaithersburg to be exact," Burked replied. "What about you?"

"I'm from right here in Atlanta. Born and raised," Hank answered. "My family settled in the north Georgia Mountains in the early eighteen-hundreds. My grandfather moved to the city when he got back from World War Two; we've been here ever since."

Burke couldn't help but steal glances at Hank's big hand resting on his thigh—a thigh threatening to burst the seams of the worn jeans the man was wearing. The bulge in the crotch of those jeans made Burke's throat go dry. He longed to run his hand along Hanks furry forearm.

"What apartment you in?" Hank asked, jerking Burke back from his fantasy.

"Fourteen-thirteen."

"Cool. You're in the building across the pool from me! Is that the second floor?" Hank asked.

"Yes. It overlooks the pool," Burke smiled. "Sparky likes the balcony."

"Double cool," Hank grinned broadly. "I think our apartments face each other!"

"Really?" Burke wasn't so sure that was such a good thing. The last thing Burke needed was to be walking around with a perpetual hard-on knowing this hunky man was so close by.

"When we get back, go out on your balcony and I'll do the same," Hank seemed excited by the prospect.

"Um, sure," Burke answered as he hoped that the apartments weren't right across from each other. "I guess I need to get back and get started unpacking."

"Understand," Hank nodded. "Moving's a bitch."

"Um, yes, it is," Burke said, standing up and calling to Sparky.

"I need to go, too," Hank followed suit. "Come on, Daisy. That laundry isn't going to do itself. Don't forget to go out on your balcony when you get back to your apartment."

"I won't," Burke assured Hank.

When he returned to his disheveled apartment, keeping his word, Burke went out onto the balcony with Sparky right on his heels. As luck would have it, Hank walked out onto his balcony about the same time, Daisy following close behind. Sure enough, Hank's apartment was right across the pool from Burke's. There couldn't have been more than a hundred and fifty feet between them.

Sparky barked a greeting to his newfound friend, and Daisy answered back. Hank waved.

"See?" Hank called out. "I figured you were right across from me."

"Great," Burke answered. *Just what I need*, he thought, as he groaned inwardly. "I'll catch you later," he said, his voice slightly echoing across the empty pool area.

Sighing heavily, Burke went back inside and started to unpack and set up his new apartment. Sparky watched as Burke went about unpacking, tackling the kitchen first. Burke had a passion for cooking, so not only was the kitchen important to him, it was also the most difficult to unpack and set up. Before he knew it, it was dusk outside and he had to turn on some lights.

Burke's stomach rumbled and Sparky's head cocked sideways. "Guess it is time to find something to eat," Burke said. Sparky agreed, jumping up spinning in circles.

Sparky had just finished chowing down when there was a knock at the door.

Opening it Burke saw Hank and Daisy, Hank with a pizza box and a twelve-pack of Heineken.

"Hey, I couldn't help but notice you hadn't stopped all day and figured you were about due for a break," Hank announced. "Thought you could use something to eat 'bout now, too."

"Um, wow...thanks." Burke was once again blown away by Hank's smile, framed by the closely trimmed beard. It was then he also noticed that he was slightly taller than Hank, putting him at about five-foot-eleven or so, compared to Burke's six-foot even.

The smell of the pizza made Burke's stomach rumble again. Standing aside, he let Hank and Daisy into the apartment. Hank set the pizza down on the kitchen counter, and held the beer out to Burke.

"I brought a bottle opener just in case you haven't found yours yet," Hank smiled broadly again.

"I've got one right here," Burke replied as he opened a drawer pulling out an opener.

"Wow, you work fast," Hank said. "It took me a week to find everything after I moved."

"I tackled the kitchen first, since it takes the most time," Burke said, as he opened two beers, handing one to Hank. He turned, putting the rest of the beer in the empty refrigerator, then opened a cabinet and took out a couple of plates.

The two men, followed by two dogs, walked into the living area of the apartment. There were several boxes stacked against one wall and a single chair and ottoman.

"Um, have a seat," Burke invited Hank to take the one chair. "I'll take the ottoman."

"Is this all the furniture you have?" Hank looked shocked as he sat in the chair.

"I did bring my mattress," Burke answered around a mouth full of pizza. "That chair was the only thing that wasn't junk, so it was the only thing I moved with me. I figured I'd pick up a few things when I got here. Cut down on the moving costs," Burked explained.

"What makes this chair so special?" Hank asked. "It is comfortable, I'll give you that."

"It is a Swedish-designed chair," Burke said. "They cost a pretty penny, but I think they're worth it."

"Well it looks like you're gonna need more than just a few things then," Hank chuckled before taking a long swig of his beer.

"True," Burke agreed. "I need to get a desk first thing. I work from home, for the most part. I will have to make an appearance at the office twice a week, though."

"What do you do?" Hank asked as Daisy sniffed at his hand hoping for a scrap.

"I do Internet security programming."

"Wow, that sounds intense." Hank looked impressed.

Burke shrugged his shoulders as if it wasn't that big a deal. "What do you do?"

"I'm a construction foreman," Hank replied. "Nothing as high tech as you."

Burke laughed. "I have a hard time with a screwdriver. Mechanical I'm not."

"Hey, don't worry; I can barely turn my computer on!" Hank said, joining in Burke's laughter. "If you need any help in putting anything together let me know, and when I need help with my computer, I'll know who to call."

"Deal," Burke smiled, knowing full well that he would need help if he had to put anything together in the near future. "Do you know of any furniture stores close by?"

"Yeah, there is this cool place not far from here, over on Sidney Marcus. They deal with all kinds of discontinued lines of furniture from all sorts of manufacturers. You can really get some good deals there."

"That sounds promising," Burke said.

"I've got some free time tomorrow. If you want, I can run you over there...show you where it is."

"I don't want to inconvenience you," Burke hesitated.

"No problem," Hank grinned. "That's what friends are for."

"Thanks for the pizza," Burke said appreciatively. "And the beer," he added holding up the near empty bottle before stifling a yawn.

"Think of it as a housewarming present," Hank answered casually. "I'll get outta here so you can get some rest."

"I am pretty beat," Burke agreed.

"Eleven work for you tomorrow?" Hank asked as he approached the door.

"That will be fine," Burke said as he opened the door. He stole a long look at Hank's very fine ass as he bent over to put the leash on Daisy. If he hadn't known better, he would have sworn that Hank took a little extra time hooking the leash to the dog harness, giving him plenty of time to admire the tight glutes.

"You got it then," Hank said, and smiled, holding out his hand. Burke took the extended hand, relishing the warm strength.

Hank said good night and left Burke and Sparky alone in the near empty apartment.

"Well there, Sparky, I'd say that Hank is about as straight as they come," Burke sighed. "Just as well, I guess. He probably won't be so friendly when he finds out I'm a fag."

Sparky looked at Burke blankly, until Burke picked up the leash.

"One more quick walk and then it's bedtime for us, boy," Burke said to Sparky, yawning again.

The next day, Hank was good to his word, showing up right at eleven. He took Burke to the store he had mentioned, and Burke was able to get a complete office suite. Unfortunately, there wasn't anything that he cared for, otherwise. The good thing was that the office furniture that he got would be delivered the next day.

Later that day, Burke passed by a boutique-type furniture store on his way to a grocery store. He liked what he saw in the window, so he stopped in and was immediately glad that he had. Burke had always been partial to the sleek Danish modern design, and this store fit his style perfectly.

He spent much more than he had planned to, but he could afford it, and it was part of his moving-on phase. After two years as a recluse, it was time to start living again. Susan, his only real friend, kept reminding him that he was still part of the human race, even if he tried to not believe it.

"Wait 'til I tell her about this," Burke smirked. "She'll flip," he said to himself as he drove back to his new apartment. For the first time in a long while—in almost a decade—Burke felt comfortable in his own skin.

The next evening, when Hank came over to help put the bookcases together, was almost Burke's undoing. Hank showed up, toolbox in hand, wearing a pair of cutoff jean shorts and a tank top. His muscular legs and arms fully exposed, the hair on his chest jutting from the top and sides of his tank top, kept Burke off balance the entire time. It didn't help matters that Burke had not been sexual with anyone but his hand since his breakup.

It was then that Burke decided that he needed to come out to Hank. The next day was Hank's birthday bash, and he wanted to give Hank the opportunity to uninvite him.

"Hey, you got any of that beer left?" Hank asked as he lifted his shirt to wipe the sweat from his forehead, exposing his furry belly to Burke's hungry eyes.

Burke's mouth went dry and suddenly the thought a cold beer for fortification sounded good. "Sure. Coming right up," he said quickly as he headed for the kitchen.

Burke was shaking slightly as he returned to the second bedroom that he was using as an office. When he got to the door of the new office with the two beers, he stopped dead in his tracks. Hank was standing there without the shirt. He was using the balled up tank top to mop his hairy armpits.

Hank looked up and saw Burke standing in the doorway, his mouth slightly open. Hank turned to face Burke.

Burke's eyes widened as he took in the muscular hairy man, muscles flexing as he moved. Although he was slightly taller than Hank, Hank probably outweighed him by at least thirty pounds, most of it muscle.

"Is one of those beers for me?" Hank asked, as he slowly walked toward Burke, a sly smirk on his face.

Not trusting his voice, Burke just stuck out one of his hands, holding a cold beer. Hank walked up to Burke and took the beer, his eyes never leaving Burke's. Burke could smell the peppery natural scent of Hank, making his head swim. He felt glued to the spot as he watched Hank lift the green glass bottle to his full lips. Hank took a long drink of the cold beer, their eyes locked. With Hank's arm lifted, his smell became that much more intense, especially since he was only standing six inches or so from Burke.

Burke took a step back, more to recover his balance than to get away from Hank. He was feeling light headed, off balance, as if he would fall over backward if he didn't regain his equilibrium.

"Somethin' the matter, Burke?" Hank asked as he propped his other arm up against the door frame, his hand shoulder level. Hank's peppery scent, tinged with a slight hint of lemon, hit Burke full force, like a slap. As if Hank's smell wasn't enough, his deep baritone voice, vibrating Burke's chest as he spoke, was the knockout punch. Hank's eyes were drilling into Burke's very being, and he felt his knees go weak. Burke could feel his mouth opening and closing, but no sound was coming out. He tried to take another step back, but his feet got tangled up in the strapping from one of the furniture boxes. With the beer in one hand, and nothing to really grab on to, Burke started falling backward. Hank reached out to try to catch him, but it was too late. Burke hit the floor, the beer bottle went flying behind him, the two dogs barking wildly, as he landed with a hard thump on the floor.

"Oh shit!" Hank was next to Burke's sprawled body in an instant. "Man, you okay?"

Burke was looking up at the ceiling, his pride hurt more than his body.

"Yeah, I'm fine," Burke grumbled, pissed at himself.

"Hey, Burke, I'm sorry man." Hank said, looking worried.

"I shouldn't have left all that trash out in the middle of the floor. I wasn't thinking."

"Don't worry about it, Hank," Burke grunted as he stood up. "I'm a natural klutz."

"You sure you're okay, man?" Hank had concern written all over his face.

"Yeah, yeah. I'll be fine," Burke grimaced as he saw the near empty beer bottle lying on the floor behind him. "Let me get that cleaned up."

"I can get it," Hank started.

"No, no...I can get it," Burke said as he went to the kitchen to get some paper towels.

"Okay," Hank sighed. "I've almost got this last bookshelf put together, but I'll need to you hold this door while I get the hinges in place."

"Sure, I'll be right there," Burke answered as he mopped up the spilt beer.

"The party is tomorrow night," Hank said screwing in the hinges as Burke held the door in place. "You're gonna be there, right?"

"Hank, I don't know," Burke started. "I won't know anyone there but you, and it's your birthday party."

"Burke, you gotta be there, man," Hank stopped, looking at Burke. "I really want you there. I can introduce you around."

There was a look in Hank's eyes that made Burke unable to say no. "Okay, Hank. I'll be there."

"Cool." Hank smiled his killer smile, making Burke immediately regret saying yes.

"I bought some more furniture and they're delivering it tomorrow, and I'm not sure what time they'll get here," Burke explained as Hank finished putting the door on the cabinet.

"I'm sure they'll be done before the party," Hank said as he tested the door. "The party doesn't start until seven."

"What do I need to bring?" Burked asked as he watched the still half-naked Hank put his tools away.

"Not a thing man. I got everything covered." The hairy man spoke through the material of his tank top as he pulled it back over his head. "It's casual, so just jeans, okay?"

"Okay, Hank," Burke said, but cringed inwardly. I'll be there."

"Cool." Hank beamed.

If he only knew what that smile did to me, Burke thought, *he would probably bash my head in.*

"Can I pay you for all this?" Burke indicated with his hand at all the stuff that Hank had put together.

"Naw, man," Burke scowled. "I may need some help with my computer next week. I'm supposed to be able to tap into the office's system to input purchase orders and stuff, and I'm not having any luck getting in."

"Sure," Burke said, finally on secure footing. "I can help with that."

"Good enough then," Hank said. "We'll call it even."

"Okay," Burke smiled, feeling much better at being able to reciprocate in some way.

"See ya tomorrow night then, buddy," Hank grabbed Burke in a one armed hug and then was out the door.

Once Hank had left the apartment, Burke put his head against the door, his eyes closed. "Holy mother of god," he whispered.

Sparky barked as in agreement.

"Yep, Sparky," Burked looked at the terrier sitting on the floor looking back at him. "I'm so screwed."

"Hey, come on in," said a man who was, well, almost Hank.

"Um...thanks," Burke stammered.

"Yeah, we get that a lot," the man said with a laugh. "Hank and I are brothers, but not twins. I'm the older and better-looking one," the *not twin* brother of Hank said as he extended his hand. "I'm Jack."

"Nice to meet you, Jack," he said, accepting Jack's hand. "I'm Burke."

"Ah, the new neighbor." Jack nodded, surprising Burke.

"Um, yeah." Burke lifted the twelve-pack of Heineken, a silent question as to where to put the beer.

"Just stick that in the fridge—if you can find room, that is." Jack smiled Hank's killer smile. "Hank! You got comp'ny," Jack yelled out over the noise, closing the door behind Burke.

"Hey, you made it," Hank exclaimed, surprising Burke with a bear hug.

"Hey," Burke said, hesitantly. "I brought a little something," he said, handing the beer to Hank.

"Thanks! Let's see if there's room in the fridge," Hank said, wrapping his big furry arm round Burke's shoulder. "If not, I've got a cooler on the balcony we can put it in." Burke could do nothing but go along.

Once in the kitchen, Hank pushed his way through the crowd of people toward the refrigerator.

"Hey, Ma," Hank said, hip-bumping an older woman in khaki slacks with salt-and-pepper hair. As she turned, there was no mistaking that she and Hank were related. "I want you to meet Burke. Burke, this is my mom."

"Very nice to meet you, Mrs. Staunton," Burke said.

"And it is very nice to meet you as well, Burke," she replied, a warm smile on her still-pretty face.

"And I'm Bitsy," a slender blonde woman interjected, as she pushed her way forward, her hand extended palm side down. "I'm an old friend of the family."

Burke noticed Hank's face go stiff, his smile suddenly forced.

"It's nice to meet you, too, Bitsy." Burke could tell instantly that he didn't like this bleached blonde. If he was correct, that wasn't the only thing that wasn't natural about this woman—her boobs and nose, for starters.

Bitsy's smile was as put-on as her makeup, Burke decided, as she wrapped her arm around Hank's waist, not unlike an anaconda.

"Ah-hum." An older man cleared his throat behind Hank's mother.

"Oh, and this is my dad," Hank introduced Burke, his smile looking genuine again.

"Nice to meet you, Mr. Staunton." Burke smiled at the warm eyes that matched Hank's.

"Same here, young man." Mr. Staunton smiled back, a twinkle in his eyes as he glanced at Hank.

Hank was able to turn out of the snake's grip that Bitsy had on him. "This is my sister Amanda," he said, hugging the female version of himself, "and my sister-in-law, Jack's wife, Heather." He kissed the cheek of a woman whose headful of curly red hair reminded Burke of a Raggedy Ann doll—in a good way.

Amanda stepped between Bitsy and Hank, extending her hand. "It is *very* nice to meet you, Burke. Hank hasn't stopped talking about you."

Burke couldn't help but blush and notice the slight scowl that flashed briefly over Bitsy's face. "It is nice to meet you all."

"Come, Burke," Mrs. Staunton said taking Burke's arm. "Let's get you something to drink. I understand that this is a joint birthday party?" Mrs. Staunton led Burke toward the balcony.

"I don't know about joint, but today is my birthday," Burke hesitantly admitted.

"Then it *is* a joint party," the older woman confirmed, smiling up at Burke.

As the party progressed, Burke noticed that at no time was he not talking with one member or another of Hank's family. There were others he was introduced to; Hank's coworkers and his or his family's other assorted friends. It was during this time that he found out that it was a family business, and that all of them worked for Knoll construction.

Burke had to admit that he was having a good time at the party, even if he was embarrassed when they all sang happy birthday to both him and Hank, insisting that he take part in blowing out the candles on the huge cake with Hank.

When Burke excused himself to go to the restroom, he overheard Bitsy talking to Hank.

"So you're telling me that you'd rather be with that fucking faggot than with *me*!"

"That's exactly what I'm telling you Bitsy," Burke heard Hank say angrily.

"But we were so good together, Hank," Bitsy whined.

"That was thirteen years ago, Bitsy." Hank sounded more exasperated now. "We were in high school, and I was confused. I'm gay, Bitsy. It's time you accepted it and got over it."

"I can make you…" she started.

"No, Bitsy, you can't," Hank said, angry again.

"Fine then." Bitsy's voice turned acid. "If you want to go be a cocksucking faggot, go right ahead, but just you wait. Wait until all the guys at work find out you like sucking dick!"

"Miss Dawson," Burke heard another man's voice. "You say one word to anyone and you will find yourself not only unemployed but I will have to have a serious talk with your father. I don't think he would be very pleased that his daughter has been fired from the construction company that contracts his heating-

and-air company." He realized the voice was Hank's father's.

Suddenly, the partially open door swung open exposing Burke as Bitsy exited the room. Spotting Burke she said, "Fucking faggot," as she pushed past him.

Hank's and Burke's eyes met.

"I think you two need to talk," Mr. Staunton said, grinning as he also saw Burke. "Excuse me."

"You're..." Burke choked before he could finish what he started to say.

Hank grabbed Burke by the arm, pulling him into the bedroom and closing the door.

"I've been trying to tell you, but I didn't know how," Hank said. "I was trying to yesterday, but when you fell..."

"You scared the shit out of me," Burke said, his voice squeaking.

"Are you scared now?"

"Yes."

"Don't be." Hank took Burke's head, his hands on either side, and slowly pulled him into a kiss. It was slow and tender, with both of their eyes wide open.

Hank ended the kiss, still looking into Burke's eyes. "Still scared?" Burke shook his head no.

"Good," Hank said, and smiled before pulling him back into another kiss, this one not so tender.

Hank slid his arms around Burke's waist, pulling him closer as his tongue pushed into Burke's mouth. Hank's fat wet tongue delved into the recesses of Burke's mouth, taking him, demanding participation.

Burke's body responded as if waking from a long hibernation, instincts taking over. He grabbed Hank's head in his hands and smashed his mouth onto those lips that he had lusted over, quickly dominating the kiss, his hips grinding into Hank's.

The door was flung open abruptly. "Here they are," Jack called out loudly over his shoulder. "They're back here swappin' spit."

"Well, good lord, close the door and let them be then, Jack," Mrs. Staunton's voice came from behind Jack.

"Way ta go, little brother." Jack smiled broadly.

"We'll see you tomorrow, Hank," Mrs. Staunton called out. "You too, Burke."

Then the door closed.

"Your family..."

"Yeah, they know," Hank whispered, his arms still around Burke's waist. "I couldn't wait for them to meet you. Kiss me again?"

It didn't take much to convince Burke when Hank moved his hands down, gripping his ass, grinding their burgeoning erections together. Burke covered Hank's mouth with his own, and this time it was his tongue doing the tonsil diving.

Something snapped inside of Burke. He growled into Hank's mouth as he started to pull Hank's Grateful Dead T-shirt up and off, giving Hank a chance to catch his breath as their lips separated. With Hank's naked chest exposed, Burke had free rein to explore the fur-covered pectorals and the erect, plum-colored nipples. He teased each sensitive nub, first by lightly pinching, then twisting, making Hank groan, his head thrown back. His hand gripping Hank's hair, Burke sucked the right nipple hard, then nibbled it, causing Hank to gasp in pain and pleasure. As Burke gave the left nipple the same treatment, Hank's hand went to the back of Burke's head, pushing harder onto the tortured nipple.

Lifting his head, Hank looked into Burke's eyes before he could kiss him again. "Please," Hank pleaded.

Releasing two years of pent-up sexual frustration, anger and just plain horniness, Burke pushed Hank back onto the bed. He reached for the fly of Hank's jeans, all but ripping them open before gripping the waistband and tugging them down and then off. Hank now lay completely naked. Burke took a moment to let his eyes explore the physical beauty lying before him: the massive chest, the tight abdomen covered in hair, the full pubic bush and then the throbbing, purple-headed dick, the head already shiny with precum. Hank's heavy balls were already slightly drawn up, making Burke's mouth water.

Standing, Burke quickly stripped off his clothes. Hank was able to take in, for the first time, Burke's tightly muscled physique. He saw what he had suspected all along, the swimmer's build he had admired clothed, now, finally, naked.

A low whine starting in the back of Burke's throat was the only notice given Hank before Burke dove between his legs, first sucking in one lightly furred egg and then the other.

White-hot flashes of light exploded in Burke's head as he tasted Hank for the first time. Inhaling deeply, he relished the musky male smell, heavy testosterone-laced pheromones filling his nostrils. In a near-frenzied state, Burke pushed Hank's legs toward his chest, exposing the furry, wrinkled hole.

Burke dove in, licking, biting and then sucking on the tight pucker, groaning, sending vibrations right into Hank, raising goose bumps on his inner thighs. He rimmed the writhing man until his tongue and throat muscles were on fire. Then he slowly worked his way up, licking and sniffing Hank as he crawled up the fuzzy body, savoring every inch. He then kissed the bearded hunk, letting him taste himself.

Hank pushed Burke off him, reached into the drawer of the nightstand and pulled out lube and a packet of condoms. He handed Burke the bottle of lube, while ripping open the foil wrapper of one of the condoms with his teeth.

Hank dropped the condom when Burke pushed a lubed finger into him. Automatically, Hank lifted his legs higher, giving Burke easy access. Burke eased the finger in and out, twisting, opening Hank up.

Hank lifted his head, looked at Burke and demanded, "In me...now," his voice a low guttural growl.

Burke withdrew his finger, and rolled the condom onto his now-painful erection. His latex-covered dick pressed against Hank's well-lubricated opening. Looking into Hank's eyes, he pushed past the tight sphincter muscle, watching Hank closely for any sign of pain.

Hank's mouth opened, but he said nothing. After a moment, he relaxed enough, allowing Burke to slowly penetrate him fully. Burke paused when he could go no farther, closed his eyes and breathed in deep, hoping not to cum right then.

Once he felt Hank push back, and when he was sure he wouldn't blow his load, he started to slowly ease himself in and out, constantly watching Hank's expression. Burke held on to Hank's ankles as he slowly built up speed.

Dropping the construction worker's ankles, bending him almost double, he pounded into him, the room echoing with the slapping of Burke's hips into Hank's hairy asscheeks. Hank's head was rolling back and forth, his eyes rolled back in his head.

Suddenly Hank lifted his head, looked into Burke's eyes and started stuttering, "I'm...can't stop...oh holy fuck..." His face turned red, the muscles on the side of his neck strained as he screamed, "I'm coming!"

Gripping his dick for the first time, Hank jacked himself twice and then unleashed a thick rope of cum, striping his body from neck to navel. He arched his back as he unloaded his dark, furry balls.

Hank's muscled ass clenched tight, making it almost impossible for Burke to move. The added tightness was enough to send Burke into orbit as he forcefully slammed his dick into Hank's hot ass.

Burke bent Hank double as he thrust his tongue and his dick into the man beneath him. Something between a scream and a growl was forced into the hirsute man's mouth as Burke continued to pummel Hank's body, filling the condom with his own blistering-hot cum.

Burke collapsed onto Hank's wet body, melding the two sweat-covered, cum-covered men together. Hank was stroking Burke's back as his dick slipped free from Hank's well-used hole.

"Talk about still waters running deep," Hank chuckled. "I knew you would be an animal in bed."

Burked lifted his head and looked at Hank as he blushed. "Um...sorry. I guess I kinda got carried away."

"Don't be sorry, I totally enjoyed it," Hank smiled, stroking the side of Burke's red face. "Let me know when you're ready to go again."

Burke smiled into those topaz eyes before replying. "Ready."

ABOUT THE AUTHORS

SHANE ALLISON is the editor of over a dozen gay erotic anthologies and has been published in just as many. He just finished his first novel and lives in Tallahassee, Florida.

BOOT LS is the author of *Erotica By Request*, writing stories for those who request them. He exists only in the world of the Internet, only as a name on the other side of stories. He is ageless, faceless, and is male only as often as he wants to be.

DAN CAVANAGH (nyc.dan7@gmail.com) has been published several times in *Drummer* and *Manifest Reader* magazines. "Of all the writers I've encountered in a long career of writing and editing gay erotica, only a handful have really pushed my own buttons, and Dan Cavanagh is foremost among them." — Aaron Travis

ERIC DEL CARLO's (ericdelcarlo.com) erotica has appeared with Circlet Press, Loose Id, Ravenous Romance, Cleis Press and other venues. He also writes science fiction and fantasy, appearing in such publications as *Asimov's* and *Strange Horizons*, and is the coauthor of the mystery novel *NO Quarter.*

LANDON DIXON's writing credits include the magazines *Men, Freshmen, [2], Mandate, Torso,* and *Honcho;* stories in the anthologies *Brief Encounters, In Plain View, Hot Jocks, Uniforms Unzipped* and *Best Gay Erotica 2009;* and the short story collections *Hot Tales of Gay Lust 1, 2* and *3.*

THOMAS FUCHS (fuchsfoxxx@cs.com) has spent much of his career writing documentary television and some print nonfiction. He greatly enjoys doing research, particularly for the erotic fiction he has recently been attempting.

CALVIN GIMPELEVICH is a compact queer of dubious virtue. His work can be found in the usual smut anthologies as well as Topside Press's *The Collection.* He lives in Seattle, Washington; but will probably, eventually, move.

Having had his first short story published in the e-zine Clean Sheets back in 2010, **TONY HAYNES** now writes regularly for X-cite books and The Big Pulp magazine. X-cite books will publish Tony's debut erotic novel, *Pleasure Island,* in Spring 2014.

LEE HITT (leehitt.wordpress.com) lives, loves and writes in New Hampshire.

DAVID HOLLY (facebook.com/david.holly2) is the author of a hundred short stories; the novels *The Moon's Deep Circle, Kissing Behind the Bathhouse* and *Stealing the Mayor's Underpants;* and the collections *The Dream in the Heart of the Forest* and *Delicious Darkness.*

For **DILO KEITH,** writing kinky erotica is the latest manifestation of a lifelong fascination with sex and multi-decadal interest in BDSM. It felt great the first time, so Dilo did it again, first alone, later with friends and eventually in public. Published works include three short stories, a novelette and academic papers.

DALE LAZAROV (dalelazarov.com) is the writer/editor of *GOOD SPORTS* (drawn by Alessio Slonimsky), *NIGHTLIFE* (drawn by Bastian Jonsson), *MANLY* (drawn by Amy Colburn), and *STICKY* (drawn by Steve MacIsaac), gay erotic comics that Gay Vox, among others, have called "the best gay erotica comics ever."

K. LYNN has been a longtime fan of the erotica market, sneaking in reading time when no one was watching. She enjoys subverting the gender stereotypes in her writing and looks forward to exploring that more in the future. When she's not writing short stories, she's working on her novels.

GREGORY L. NORRIS (gregorylnorris.blogspot.com) writes full time from the Outer Limits of New Hampshire and is the author of the handbook to all-things-Sunnydale, *The Q Guide to Buffy the Vampire Slayer* (Alyson Books) and the recent *The Fierce and Unforgiving Muse: Twenty-Six Tales From the Terrifying Mind of Gregory L. Norris* (EJP).

HUCK PILGRIM (huckpilgrim.wordpress.com) is the pseudonym of a minor author who craves readers, and doesn't mind working hard on his books. He is a father and a husband, enjoys his family, writing, and watching movies. Self-publishing erotic ebooks is his latest foolish pursuit.

JASON A. QUEST (JAQrabbit.com) aspires to be a professional pornographer and heretic. He writes and draws religious satire under the *Holy Comics!* imprint, and is working on a quasi-autobio-porno-graphic novel *JAQrabbit Tales,* a bisexual man's life story told through sex scenes, illustrated by himself and various artists.

DOMINIC SANTI is a former technical editor turned rogue whose smutty stories have appeared in dozens of anthologies, including *Wild Boys, Hot Daddies, Uniforms Unzipped, Beach Bums, Gay Quickies, Sexy Sailors, Middle Men, Pledges,* and several volumes of *Best Gay Erotica.* Plans include an even dirtier historical novel.

J. M. SNYDER (jms-books.com) writes gay erotic/romantic fiction and has worked with many different publishers over the years. Snyder's short stories have appeared in anthologies by Alyson Books and Cleis Press. In 2010, Snyder founded JMS Books LLC, a queer small press, which publishes GLBT fiction, nonfiction and poetry.

Residing on English Bay in Vancouver, Canada, **JAY STARRE** has pumped out steamy gay fiction for dozens of anthologies and has written two gay erotic novels.

MAX VOS is a classically trained chef with over thirty years of food service experience. After retiring in 2011, Max found himself with time on his hands and turned his talents to writing. "Cooking English," a short story, was his first published work. He has just completed his first novel.

ABOUT THE EDITORS

LARRY DUPLECHAN is the author of five acclaimed gay novels, including *Blackbird* (1985) and the Lambda Literary Award-winning *Got 'til It's Gone* (2008). He served as guest judge for *Best Gay Erotica 2012* and is honored to continue the BGE series as editor. Larry lives in a suburb of Los Angeles with his husband of thirty-seven years and their Chartreux cat, Mr. Blue. His erotic art can be found at ChoklitDaddysSketchbook. blogspot.com.

JOE MANNETTI is an actor and LGBT activist. He obtained a Bachelor of Arts degree in literature while living in New York. He is probably most publicly identified for his multiple Bear titles, including Mr. International Daddy Bear 2009, and for his work in erotic videos performing as "Joe Falconi." Joe currently resides just outside of New York.

Best Erotica Series

"Gets racier every year."—San Francisco Bay Guardian

Buy 4 books,
Get 1 *FREE**

Best Women's Erotica 2013
Edited by Violet Blue
ISBN 978-1-57344-898-7 $15.95

Best Women's Erotica 2012
Edited by Violet Blue
ISBN 978-1-57344-755-3 $15.95

Best Women's Erotica 2011
Edited by Violet Blue
ISBN 978-1-57344-423-1 $15.95

Best Bondage Erotica 2013
Edited by Rachel Kramer Bussel
ISBN 978-1-57344-897-0 $15.95

Best Bondage Erotica 2012
Edited by Rachel Kramer Bussel
ISBN 978-1-57344-754-6 $15.95

Best Bondage Erotica 2011
Edited by Rachel Kramer Bussel
ISBN 978-1-57344-426-2 $15.95

Best Lesbian Erotica 2013
Edited by Kathleen Warnock.
Selected and introduced by
Jewelle Gomez.
ISBN 978-1-57344-896-3 $15.95

Best Lesbian Erotica 2012
Edited by Kathleen Warnock.
Selected and introduced by
Sinclair Sexsmith.
ISBN 978-1-57344-752-2 $15.95

Best Lesbian Erotica 2011
Edited by Kathleen Warnock.
Selected and introduced by Lea DeLaria.
ISBN 978-1-57344-425-5 $15.95

Best Gay Erotica 2013
Edited by Richard Labonté.
Selected and introduced by Paul Russell.
ISBN 978-1-57344-895-6 $15.95

Best Gay Erotica 2012
Edited by Richard Labonté.
Selected and introduced by
Larry Duplechan.
ISBN 978-1-57344-753-9 $15.95

Best Gay Erotica 2011
Edited by Richard Labonté.
Selected and introduced by
Kevin Killian.
ISBN 978-1-57344-424-8 $15.95

Best Fetish Erotica
Edited by Cara Bruce
ISBN 978-1-57344-355-5 $15.95

Best Bisexual Women's Erotica
Edited by Cara Bruce
ISBN 978-1-57344-320-3 $15.95

Best Lesbian Bondage Erotica
Edited by Tristan Taormino
ISBN 978-1-57344-287-9 $16.95

★ Free book of equal or lesser value. Shipping and applicable sales tax extra.
Cleis Press • (800) 780-2279 • orders@cleispress.com
www.cleispress.com

The Bestselling Novels of James Lear

Buy 4 books, Get 1 FREE*

The Mitch Mitchell Mystery Series

The Back Passage
By James Lear

"Lear's lusty homage to the classic whodunit format (sorry, Agatha) is wonderfully witty, mordantly mysterious, and enthusiastically, unabashedly erotic!"
—Richard Labonté,
Book Marks, Q Syndicate
ISBN 978-1-57344-423-5 $13.95

The Secret Tunnel
By James Lear

"Lear's prose is vibrant and colourful...This isn't porn accompanied by a wahwah guitar, this is porn to the strains of Beethoven's *Ode to Joy*, each vividly realised ejaculation accompanied by a fanfare and the crashing of cymbals."—*Time Out London*
ISBN 978-1-57344-329-6 $15.95

A Sticky End
A Mitch Mitchell Mystery
By James Lear

To absolve his best friend and sometime lover from murder charges, Mitch races around London finding clues while bedding the many men eager to lend a hand—or more.
ISBN 978-1-57344-395-1 $14.95

The Low Road
By James Lear

Author James Lear expertly interweaves spies and counterspies, scheming servants and sadistic captains, tavern trysts and prison orgies into this delightfully erotic work.
ISBN 978-1-57344-364-7 $14.95

Hot Valley
By James Lear

"Lear's depiction of sweaty orgies...trumps his Southern war plot, making the violent history a mere inconsequential backdrop to all of Jack and Aaron's sticky mischief. Nice job."
—*Bay Area Reporter*
ISBN 978-1-57344-279-4 $14.95

★ **Free book of equal or lesser value. Shipping and applicable sales tax extra.**
Cleis Press • (800) 780-2279 • orders@cleispress.com
www.cleispress.com

Men on the Make

**Buy 4 books,
Get 1 FREE***

Wild Boys
Gay Erotic Fiction
Edited by Richard Labonté

Take a walk on the wild side with these fierce tales of rough trade. Defy the rules and succumb to the charms of hustlers, jocks, kinky tricks, smart-asses, con men, straight guys and gutter punks who give as good as they get.
ISBN 978-1-57344-824-6 $15.95

Sexy Sailors
Gay Erotic Stories
Edited by Neil Plakcy

Award-winning editor Neil Plakcy has collected bold stories of naughty, nautical hunks and wild, stormy sex that are sure to blow your imagination.
ISBN 978-1-57344-822-2 $15.95

Hot Daddies
Gay Erotic Fiction
Edited by Richard Labonté

From burly bears and hunky father figures to dominant leathermen, *Hot Daddies* captures the erotic dynamic between younger and older men: intense connections, consensual submission, and the toughest and tenderest of teaching and learning.
ISBN 978-1-57344-712-6 $14.95

Straight Guys
Gay Erotic Fantasies
Edited by Shane Allison

Gaybie Award-winner Shane Allison shares true and we-wish-they-were-true stories in his bold collection. From a husband on the down low to a muscle-bound footballer, from a special operations airman to a redneck daddy, these men will sweep you off your feet.
ISBN 978-1-57344-816-1 $15.95

Cruising
Gay Erotic Stories
Edited by Shane Allison

Homemade glory holes in a stall wall, steamy shower trysts, truck stop rendezvous…According to Shane Allison, "There's nothing that gets the adrenaline flowing and the muscle throbbing like public sex."
ISBN 978-1-57344-795-7 $14.95

* **Free book of equal or lesser value. Shipping and applicable sales tax extra.**
Cleis Press • (800) 780-2279 • orders@cleispress.com
www.cleispress.com

Rousing, Arousing
Adventures with Hot Hunks

**Buy 4 books,
Get 1 *FREE****

The Riddle of the Sands
By Geoffrey Knight

Will Professor Fathom's team of gay adventure-hunters un-
cover the legendary Riddle of the Sands in time to save one
of their own? Is the Riddle a myth, a mirage, or the greatest
engineering feat in the history of ancient Egypt? "A thrill-a-
page romp, a rousing, arousing adventure for queer boys-at-
heart men."—Richard Labonté, Book Marks
ISBN 978-1-57344-366-1 $14.95

Divas Las Vegas
By Rob Rosen

Filled with action and suspense, hunky blackjack dealers, divine drag queens,
strange sex, and sex in strange places, plus
a Federal agent or two, *Divas Las Vegas* puts
the sin in Sin City.
ISBN 978-1-57344-369-2 $14.95

The Back Passage
By James Lear

Blackmail, police corruption, a dizzying
network of spy holes and secret passages,
and a nonstop queer orgy backstairs and
everyplace else mark this hilariously hard-
core mystery by a major new talent.
ISBN 978-1-57344-423-5 $13.95

The Secret Tunnel
By James Lear

"Lear's prose is vibrant and colourful...This
isn't porn accompanied by a wah-wah guitar, this is porn to the strains of Beethoven's
Ode to Joy, each vividly realised ejaculation
accompanied by a fanfare and the crashing
of cymbals."—*Time Out London*
ISBN 978-1-57344-329-6 $15.95

A Sticky End
A Mitch Mitchell Mystery
By James Lear
To absolve his best friend and sometimes
lover from murder charges, Mitch races
around London finding clues while bedding the many men eager to lend a hand—
or more.
ISBN 978-1-57344-395-1 $14.95

*** Free book of equal or lesser value. Shipping and applicable sales tax extra.
Cleis Press • (800) 780-2279 • orders@cleispress.com
www.cleispress.com**

More from Shane Allison

Buy 4 books, Get 1 FREE*

College Boys
Gay Erotic Stories
Edited by Shane Allison
First feelings of lust for another boy, all-night study sessions, the excitement of a student hot for a teacher...is it any wonder that college boys are the objects of fantasy the world over?
ISBN 978-1-57344-399-9 $14.95

Hot Cops
Gay Erotic Stories
Edited by Shane Allison
"From smooth and fit to big and hairy... it's like a downtown locker room where everyone has some sort of badge."—*Bay Area Reporter*
ISBN 978-1-57344-277-0 $14.95

Frat Boys
Gay Erotic Stories
Edited by Shane Allison
ISBN 978-1-57344-713-3 $14.95

Brief Encounters
69 Hot Gay Shorts
Edited by Shane Allison
ISBN 978-1-57344-664-8 $15.95

Backdraft
Fireman Erotica
Edited by Shane Allison
"Seriously: This book is so scorching hot that you should box it with a fire extinguisher and ointment. It will burn more than your fingers." —*Tucson Weekly*
ISBN 978-1-57344-325-8 $14.95

Afternoon Pleasures
Erotica for Gay Couples
Edited by Shane Allison
ISBN 978-1-57344-658-7 $14.95

Hard Working Men
Gay Erotic Fiction
Edited by Shane Allison
ISBN 978-1-57344-406-4 $14.95

* Free book of equal or lesser value. Shipping and applicable sales tax extra.
Cleis Press • (800) 780-2279 • orders@cleispress.com
www.cleispress.com

Ordering is easy! Call us toll free or fax us to place your MC/VISA order.
You can also mail the order form below with payment to:
Cleis Press, 2246 Sixth St., Berkeley, CA 94710.

ORDER FORM

QTY	TITLE	PRICE
_____	_____	_____
_____	_____	_____
_____	_____	_____
_____	_____	_____
_____	_____	_____
_____	_____	_____
_____	_____	_____
_____	_____	_____

	SUBTOTAL	_____
	SHIPPING	_____
	SALES TAX	_____
	TOTAL	_____

Add $3.95 postage/handling for the first book ordered and $1.00 for each additional book. Outside North America, please contact us for shipping rates. California residents add 9% sales tax. Payment in U.S. dollars only.

* Free book of equal or lesser value. Shipping and applicable sales tax extra.

Cleis Press • Phone: (800) 780-2279 • Fax: (510) 845-8001
orders@cleispress.com • www.cleispress.com
You'll find more great books on our website

Follow us on Twitter @cleispress • Friend/fan us on Facebook